LOS ANGELES UNIFIED SCHOOL DISTRICT

HIGH SCHOOL TEXTBOOK

This book is the property of the Los Angeles Unified School District, and should receive the best of care. Settlement for damages beyond ordinary wear must be made when book is returned. Fill in the following information on first blank below: Date (month and year), teacher's name, pupil's signature and room number.

Date Mo./Year	TEACHER	PUPIL	Room No.

FORM 34-H-129 REV. 4/94 (STK. NO. 9661225775)

after HAMELIN

Bill Richardson

ANNICK PRESS LTD.

TORONTO • NEW YORK • VANCOUVER

Fifth printing, September 2002

We acknowledge the support of the Canada Council for the Arts, the Ontario Arts Council, and the Government of Canada through the Book Publishing Industry Development Program (BPIDP) for our publishing activities.

Edited by Barbara Pulling
Copyedited by Elizabeth McLean
Cover art by Charles Bell
Cover and interior design by Irvin Cheung/iCheung Design

Cataloguing in Publication Data

Richardson, Bill, 1955–
After Hamelin

ISBN 1-55037-629-2 (bound) ISBN 1-55037-628-4 (pbk.)

I. Title.
PS8585.I186A77 2000 jC813'.54 C00-930238-7
PZ7.R52Af 2000

The art in this book was rendered digitally.
The text was typeset in Granjon and Democratica.

Distributed in Canada by
Firefly Books Ltd.
3680 Victoria Park Avenue
Willowdale, ON
M2H 3K1

Distributed in the USA by
Firefly Books (U.S.) Inc.
P.O. Box 1338
Ellicott Station
Buffalo, NY 14205

Published in the USA by
Annick Press (U.S.) Ltd.

Printed and bound in Canada

visit us at **www.annickpress.com**

This book is dedicated to Barbara Nichol, with affection and admiration;
and to anyone who has ever been left behind.

Contents

LEGEND

The legend of the Pied Piper is very old. There are many different versions of the story, but all of them tell how a mysterious piper in piebald clothing was hired to rid the town of Hamelin of its rats. When the townspeople refused to pay the piper as they had promised, he took revenge by piping away the children. One child, unable to follow the piper's tune, was left behind.

This book tells the story of that child. The Pied Piper legend comes from the Middle Ages, and Hamelin is a real town in the country we now call Germany, but this story is not tied to those particulars. It unfolds in a place that isn't here and a time that isn't now.

Between living and dreaming, there is a third thing. Guess it.

— *Antonio Machado*

Section 1

once upon a time

I

who I am

I am Penelope. It is an easy name to remember. Even so, the people in this village seem to have entirely forgotten it. They call me "the funny old lady in the house with the harps." I speak of the grownups. Children call me "Harpy," for short. The little boys also like to call me "Scarface."

"Harpy, Harpy, Scarface!" they bellow, whenever they see me coming down the cobbled road, or when they scurry past me in the crowded market, shouting and scattering oranges and onions as they knock against the barrows.

One of them is especially villainous. Mellon. The ringleader. It is Mellon who leads the cruel taunting.

"Harpy, Harpy, Scarface, with her frizzy, fuzzy hair,
Harpy, Harpy, Scarface, she's as ugly as a bear!

It's vexing. There are days, especially when my joints are sore and someone has aimed a kick at my cane, that I would happily see them all turned into rats. I could arrange it. Fix it up. And maybe I will. Maybe one day, before too long, I'll do just that.

"Harpy, Harpy, Scarface!" they holler, and I imagine how they would look with tails and whiskers and pink little twitchy noses.

One day I would like to corral the little louts and show them a harpy. They would quickly understand that harpies and I have nothing in common. One good look at the genuine item would make that clear. It would also cure them of their rudeness, which no one would call a bad thing.

"Harpy, Harpy, Scarface!" I do not hear them say it. I see it. I read the words on their lips as they charge by, for though I am 101 years old I am proud to say that my eyes are still bright. A hundred and one years old! I have been deaf for ninety years. Deaf for longer than most people have been alive. For that whole time I have heard the world through my eyes. I have seen many more stories than I could ever hope to tell.

What I set before you here is the one tale I would not see forgotten. It is important that I do this now, while my memory is still unfogged. Lately, it has taken to misting over. Just last night, as I was getting ready for bed, I lost the word "comb." I was fixing my hair, which is as white as you would expect for someone of my age, and miraculously thick and unruly. I looked for it on my vanity table, the comb I mean, and didn't see it. I thought, Where is my——? But there was only a blank space where "comb" should have been.

I think of the thousands of words I might have called to mind just then. Elephant. Banana. Jackknife. Parapet. But the one word I needed was not to be found. I took a deep breath. I shut my eyes. And of course, it returned. Comb! It was gone but a second or two. Well. Such things happen. The mind plays tricks, even on young people. Still, it left me rattled. I shook my head and opened my eyes. I looked in my mirror. I saw the reflection of something dark, a thick shadow, pass through the room and slip away under the door. It disappeared, and the room went chill.

Morning came. The sun rose, all brassy and polished. This new day is warm, but I can't shake the shiver the shadow left behind. It was not just passing through. It had a reason. It was a warning. No one lives 101 years if she is heedless of such signs. It was telling me that the time has come for Penelope to write down where she went. What she saw. What she remembers. And so I will. So now I will begin.

2

The Last Sounds

I remember the last sounds I ever heard, all those years ago. They were sounds both sweet and sad. This was on my birthday eve, on the night before I would turn eleven. The rats were three months gone. Our fat cat, Scallywaggle, was restless and bored. Scally was two years older than I, and until the day the rats were piped away he had always had a job to do. There had always been rats to keep him amused.

Rats, rats, rats. While other towns were celebrated for their cheeses or churches, for their festivals or frescoes, Hamelin was famous for its rats. Not for the beauty of its rats. Not for the agility of its rats. Not for the intelligence of its rats. It was only their numbers that made the rats impressive. They were everywhere. In the pantry, in the vestry, in the sheds, under the beds, in the steeple clocks, in the chimney pots, behind the walls and in the halls: anywhere you cared to look, you could count on finding a rat.

Rats, rats, rats. No one could remember a time before the

Plague. That was what we called the ratty infestation. The Plague. As near as anyone could recall, the rats had always been there. They were as much a part of Hamelin as the streets or the air.

Only for a cat with Scally's gifts was this paradise. Never was there a more devoted sentry. Morning, noon and night he was on the lookout for the glint of beady eye and the whisk of hairless tail. His keen, soft ears were forever tuned to the sound of the rats' pit pat, as they scurried along the rafters or through the thatch of the roof. Scally was plump, but he was nimble. What's more, he was merciless. My father, the great harper Govan, wrote this song to praise him.

There is no cat like Scally
He'll never dilly dally
He'll sight a rat and rodent blood will spill.
Each morning forth he'll sally
To up his total tally
He'll bare his claws and teeth and make his kill.
Sing hey ho, Scallywaggle, how the rats drop!
Sing hi ho, Scallywaggle, snicker snack chop!

"Scally has changed," I said to my mother. Her name was Ebba. She was sitting by my bed on that evening of my last day of being ten. The last night of my hearing. Scally had taken up his usual position, on the pillow next to my head. During the night, it was his habit to inch over until he was directly atop my crown. He was like a wig with four paws. My sister, Sophy, called him a calico hat.

"Changed?" Ebba smiled as she bent down to kiss me and stroke my hair. It was red in those days, and had a will of its own. I tried to discipline it by wearing it in tightly woven plaits, but it was too independent to stay locked up. Stray, frizzy ends were always escaping. I looked like an exploding seed pod. Mother picked up one of my crazy braids and teased fat Scally with the ribbon. He gave it a half-hearted bat, breathed a deep purr that was almost a snore, then closed his eyes.

"Haven't you noticed? He's become so much slower. It's as if he's rusted."

"Scally is thirteen, Penelope."

"So is Sophy, but she only gets bouncier and bouncier."

Sophy, who was as beautiful as I was plain, had started to sprout breasts. They fascinated her. She was as proud of them as if they were something she'd worked for or earned. As if they were prize tomatoes she'd coaxed out of rocky ground.

"For a cat," said my mother, deliberately ignoring my cheekiness, "thirteen is quite old. You can't expect him to keep acting like a kitten."

"I know. But it's not just older. He's sadder, too."

"Ratting kept Scally happy and spry. Now the Plague is over, and Scally has lost his occupation. Perhaps that's as difficult for a cat as it is for a human."

She was doing her best to be cheerful, but I could sense her sadness. It was always there, just under the surface of her voice. She looked over her shoulder and through the doorway to the kitchen where my father sat on his stool by the fire. It was summer—my birthday is July 8—and the night was almost hot. Even so, Govan could not stay warm enough. Ever since he had fallen ill, a chill had been his constant companion. He huddled close to the hearth. On his lap, he held a small harp. He fingered a slow and melancholy tune, a song about a mother bird who comes home to find her nest is empty. Where, she wonders, have her babies gone?

Sophy was at the window. Illumined by the last sunlight, she was more beautiful than ever. She stood weaving willow wands into a basket. I am 101 years old, and I remember all this. I see it so clearly I might as well be in the room. I see blind Alloway, sitting on a low stool next to his master. Alloway came to our house as Govan's apprentice and simply stayed. Over the years, he had become part of our family. I remember that Govan sighed with pain and stopped his playing. He passed his apprentice the harp, and Alloway took up the tune. I remember all this, and I remember how, on the last night of my hearing, Ebba turned back and leaned down to kiss me, five times. That was our nightly ritual. Forehead. Cheek. Chin. Cheek. Forehead. She called this her charmed circle. Every night she conjured with her kisses a place where only angels could enter. Her lips brushed over my forehead and I felt a tear fall on my brow.

"Mother?"

"Hush. It's nothing. I'm silly with tears. There should be no sadness on your last night of being ten. Tomorrow is an important day for you, Penelope. You must think good thoughts. Have sweet dreams. Now, good night."

I closed my eyes. I listened to the night. Outside, there were crickets. A nightingale, far away. A horse and cart rattling slowly down the street. Inside, there was the low rumble of Scallywaggle, lying by my head. There was the lulling burble of the kettle on the fire, and the hiss and pop of the embers. There was Alloway's measured playing, and Sophy's soft singing.

Now has come the evening
When all God's creatures rest.
Now has come a mother thrush
Returning to her nest.
Now has come a mother thrush
To find her babies gone.
All her pretty feathered ones
Have taken wing and flown.
All her pretty feathered ones
Have taken to the sky.
My heart is broken, cries the thrush,
I fear that I may die.
She sings her last, most mournful song.
It echoes far and near.
Then tucks her head beneath her wing
And sheds a final tear.

Cat, cricket, cart. Hearth, harp, home. The last sounds I was ever to hear. When morning came, everything would be changed. My world would be silent. And I would never be ten again.

3

skipping and elevening

When you are 101 years old, the past becomes more interesting than the future. For one thing, there is so much more of it. When you are 101 years old, you know for a fact that the future is something you don't have plenty of.

I think about the past all the time. It was a better time than the present. Or so I believe. It makes me sad to see how much has been lost. Take jumping rope, for example. When I was a girl, we were skippers. Nan and Elfleda. Bridget and Newlyn. Petra, Osmanna, and Ninnoc and Rayne. I remember those girls. Their red cheeks. Their flying plaits. Their clear, singing voices as they skipped and sang the many rhymes we all knew.

Nip and Tuck are tailors,
Dip and Duck are sailors.
Skip around the steeple
Till you come back home!

Those songs were a part of us. We sang them when we skipped alone. We sang them when we skipped in a pack. Forward skip, backward skip, fancy skip, plain skip, we sang them all the time.

Skip around the garden
Skip around the shed
Skip around the kitchen
Skip around the bed

Skip around the flagpole
Skip around the shop
Skip and skip and skip and skip
And skip until you drop!

They were the same songs our mothers sang, and that their mothers sang before them. They were good old songs, too. Now they are forgotten. It might still happen, as I creak along to the market, that I'll see a girl or two jumping rope. But I read no words on their lips. Now, they skip in silence. I would like to tell them about the way it was. That I was the best skipper in all of Hamelin. That when I was a girl I could jump a thousand turns and not even be puffing. I would like to tell them all that and more, but I know they would just laugh at me. Daft old harpy. Living in the past.

Perhaps I *am* daft. In many ways it is better for girls today than it was when I was a child. For one thing, they have never had to live with a plague of rats. For another, they go to school. In my day, schooling belonged to the boys. In my day, it was quite unusual for a girl to know how to read. Sophy and I did. Ebba had fought with her father to learn how, and she was determined that her daughters would also know. She and Govan taught us at home. But many of our friends could scarcely repeat the alphabet. They could not write their names.

Mostly, it was the boys who learned to read and write. It was the boys who learned arithmetic and geography. All that belonged to girls alone was skipping and elevening.

You have heard of elevening, of course. It happens still on a girl's eleventh birthday, but it is just a shadow of what it was.

Today, when a girl is elevened, she will have a party and a cake. Often, the cake will have a fortune written in icing. *You will have much happiness. You will be a great beauty. The world will be your oyster.* I see such cakes in the baker's window. They make me sad, for when I was a girl there was much more to elevening than a cake with a made-up fortune. It was the day you waited for all your young life. The beginning of your life as a woman. Much fuss. Much feasting. And it was on the day you turned eleven that you were taken to visit Cuthbert.

Cuthbert was a wise man. A hermit. He lived deep in the woods, in a simple hut. His sole companion was a three-legged dog named Ulysses. His only visitors were the elevening girls who came calling with their mothers. Cuthbert would tell them their fortunes. He would look into tea leaves, look into their palms, consult his crystal ball. It was said he could see into the future. He would speak to each girl of what was to come. He would tell her about her particular gift, the special talent that made her unique in the world. Hearing the news about your gift was the most important part of your elevening day. It had been that way for generations.

"How old is he?" I asked Ebba one day, not long before my birthday.

"Cuthbert? No one knows. Ageless, I suppose."

"How is that possible?"

"With Cuthbert, what is simply is."

"What would happen if he died before my elevening?"

"Penelope!"

"Well, he might."

"He won't."

"Does he look the same now as he did when you were elevened?"

"He hasn't changed a jot."

"And was he right?"

"About what?"

"About your future. About your gift."

"How often have I told you that?"

"Tell me again!"

"He told me I would know joy and sorrow both."

"And have you?"

"Some of each, as everyone will."

"What else?"

"He told me I would raise extraordinary children. And he told me I had the gift of patience. Which, I might add, is a good thing, when one of my extraordinary children asks so many questions."

Extraordinary. I knew it was so of Sophy. She was beautiful. She sang like an angel. But there was nothing much that I could do, other than skip circles around every other girl in Hamelin. And could that be my gift? Skipping? Surely not. It certainly wasn't extraordinary. Not in any way that mattered.

Five and two is seven,
Two and nine's eleven.
What will Cuthbert tell me
When the big day comes?

Elevening. Like any other girl of my time, I couldn't wait for it to happen. Every night, I would think about the way it would all be. I would strain my eyes to look into the future. Had I known even a little of everything that was to happen, I would have prayed for time to stop, or to take me backwards instead. But time went on. And before I knew it, the day of my elevening was upon me.

4

The Harper's Daughter

Hemlock, beech and cherry
Fit them out with strings.
Oak and ash and poplar
Can all be made to sing.
Skip the harper's daughter,
Skip where you will roam,
Skip the harper's daughter
And skip your way back home!

I am a harper's daughter. In our house, for as long as I could remember, the thrum and ring of the harp had been as common a sound as the clatter of dishes or the slamming of a door. Everyone knew there was no harper finer than my father. Banquets, festivals, state occasions: none would be complete if the virtuoso Govan were not on hand to strike the harp.

His fame was widespread. Apprentices came from near and far to study with him. There was always a young man staying in our attic room. Sometimes, if they were homesick, they would talk in their sleep. I would wake in the night and hear them moaning sad-sounding words in Italian, Spanish, Welsh, Portuguese. Not even the Plague kept them away. They were willing to put up with rats gnawing their shoes and chewing their strings so they might learn to play, and also learn how to make the harps for which my father was so celebrated.

From far and near they came, with all their talent and all their yearning. But no one, no matter how gifted, was able to convince a harp to sing as true as Govan. And no one, no matter how diligently he worked, was able to make a harp with a voice as pure as one crafted by the master. The Maestro. That is what they called Govan. The Maestro. He could charm the music out of wood. No one, Govan least of all, could explain how he awakened the melody in balsam or beech or fir.

"The gifts we are born with are mysterious," he told me once, "and it is best not to ask too many questions. Our duty is to accept them and to use them. And of course, we must be thankful for them. Many gifts have wilted because of ingratitude."

"But what if you're not given any gifts?"

"Everyone is given at least one."

"Then what is mine?"

Govan smiled.

"You'll know soon enough. The day of your elevening will come. You'll be a woman. And time will fly by, and before you know it, you'll be married. And then you'll make me a grandfather. And I will teach your sons to play the harp. To build them, too, if they have the feel for the wood."

I wanted to ask, "And what about me? Could I learn to make harps, too?" For that was what I longed to do, more than anything else. I didn't hanker after playing the instrument. I adored the sounds my father could stroke from it, but I knew very well that music-making didn't live in me the same way it did in Sophy. That was her gift, not mine.

No, it was the instrument itself I loved. Its broad and vibrating back. The elegant swell of its breast. The flat plane of its strings. Just as Sophy stuck close to Ebba while our mother was baking bread or preparing a soup, so I would sit near my father, quietly watching him carve and plane and bend his wood. I loved seeing how the individual pieces were measured and made, then joined together to make the frame without so much as a single nail. I loved the smell of the freshly mixed varnish he would slather on the harp, and loved just as much the way he could take raw gut and spin it into strings. It fascinated me that what came from the insides of a sheep could be made to sound like the breathing of angels. Govan concentrated so furiously on his work and on supervising his apprentices that he often forgot I was there. He would look up to see me, and an expression first of surprise and then of remembrance would cross his face.

"My little harp maker," he would say, jokingly, and I would always smile back at him. He had no idea how much my fingers itched to do that work. To use those chisels, picks and knives. I never asked if he would teach me. What was the point? Govan was a man. His apprentices were boys. The harp belonged to them. It always had. I knew this, but still I harbored a foolish hope: Cuthbert. My secret wish was that, on the day of my elevening, when Ebba took me to see him, he would look at my hands. He would look into my eyes. He would read his crystal ball. He would shake his head. Then he would say, "I have never seen anything like this before. This is a girl whose gift is one of harp-building. Most unusual. From this day forward, she must be both her father's daughter and his apprentice."

As it turned out, Cuthbert did have something surprising to tell me. But it was stranger than anything I could ever have imagined.

5

The Arrival of Alloway

By the time you reach 101, you will have learned many lessons. For instance, you will have learned that almost nothing turns out according to plan. And you will know that when we get what we wish for, it is often because we have followed a twisty path. You have only to look at me to see the truth of what I'm saying. For in the end, I did become a harp maker. As for the journey that took me there—well, it was anything but common.

By the time of my elevening, everything had changed for Govan and for our family. It began with a stiffness that settled on him slowly. At first, his toes were swollen and sore. As time went by, the pain claimed his ankles, knees and hips. His knuckles grew big as acorns. Once, his hands had been a blur as they jumped nimbly over the strings. But there were no more spritely jigs and reels after the stiffness entered his fingers. Slow laments were all he could manage. There were days when even those were too much to bear.

Word of his illness spread. In Italy, Spain, Wales and

Portugal they learned that the Maestro had lost his famous touch. No more apprentices came to the door. Only Alloway remained. Alloway, whose accent was pure Hamelin, as this is where he was born and where he had always lived. Alloway, who came into the world blind and whose parents left him naked and squalling on the steps of the foundling home. Alloway, who had nowhere else to go, and who could never imagine living under a roof other than ours. We were the only family he knew. What was more, he had fallen deeply, irretrievably in love with Sophy.

"Why do you love her?" I asked him once, when we were alone and I felt bold.

"She is beautiful."

"But how do you know? You can't see her."

"I can tell by the brush of her skirt on the floor. I can tell by her laugh. I can tell by the way the air changes when she walks into the room. And I can tell by the way she sings."

"Govan says that even the rocks and the trees fall in love with Sophy when she sings."

"Yes. That is her gift."

Alloway. I remember when he came to us. It was a bitter January day, sunless and icy. You couldn't see across the road through the curtain of hard, black sleet. I was five by then, and it was I who heard the knock and opened the door.

"Is your father here, girl?"

I knew the man on the threshold. He was the director of the Hamelin orphanage. The drenched and skinny boy in raggedy clothes who huddled beside him, quivering with cold, I had never seen. His hair was wilder even than mine, dark and heavy with water. An icicle hung from his nose. I tried to meet his stare but couldn't. His eyes were vacant. They took nothing in. They gave no light back.

My mother fed the boy broth. He slurped it with loud gusto. Sophy and I hid under the table. We listened to our father and the orphanage man.

"So you see my situation, Govan. The boy will soon turn ten. He can't stay with us forever. We are overcrowded as it is. It is time he learned a trade, but no one will have him."

"Why have you brought him to me?"

"Is it not true that blind boys can be taught to play the harp?"

"There have been many blind harpers. Sight is not a requirement if your fingers have a feel for the strings. But unless the boy has music in him, there is very little I could do for him. If music doesn't live in his head and his heart, I could no more teach him to play than I could teach him to plow a field or milk a cow. Does he sing?"

"Sing? Oh, surely. Boy!"

Alloway turned his head toward the director's bark.

"Give us a tune!"

Until then, Alloway had not uttered a sound. He held onto his mug, and his shoulders sagged.

"We haven't got all night. Sing!"

The bleat that fell from his lips! Sophy and I clapped our hands over our mouths to keep from laughing.

"Thank you, Alloway," said Govan. And to the orphanage man he said, "Yes. It is surely a remarkable voice. Tremendous —volume. Of course, he must stay here with us."

And from that moment onward, he did.

"Why, Govan?" I heard Ebba say that night, when we were in bed and they thought we were asleep. "He's a lovely boy, I'm sure, and I pity him for his blindness. But there's no more music in him than there is in the cat."

"He was brought here for a reason. I feel it in my bones. Besides, there may be more music in him than we think."

Govan was right. While people would never flock to hear him sing, in time Alloway found one or two pleasing notes in his voice. He learned his way around the harp well enough. He proved also to have a talent for mimicry; and he never failed to make us laugh with his impersonations. Alloway became part of our family, and the day would come that we'd understand how lucky we were he was sent to us.

6

My Dream of the Dancing Rats

Some people claim that they never dream. This is nonsense. Everyone dreams. What's true is that some remember their dreams better than others. Mine I have always recalled in their every detail. Sometimes, my dreamtime remembering is so vivid that I'm not sure what belongs to the world of sleep and what belongs to the world of waking. People who lose their dreams the moment they open their eyes often envy those of us whose memories are keen. The forgetters think they are missing out on something. They think the extravagant dreamers somehow have richer lives. And perhaps, in some ways, we do.

But there have been times—many times, in fact—when I would have welcomed absentmindedness. What good did it do me, when I was only ten, that the rats were gone from the streets of Hamelin when every night they built their nests in my dreams? It was always the same. I shut my eyes. Sleep came knocking. I let him in. He would take me by the elbow and usher me back to that terrible world of before the Piper came. Rats were everywhere, then. They were even in our skipping songs.

Rats under pillows and rats in our boots,
Rats in the willows from branches to roots,
Rats brown and spotted, rats black and white,
Rats in the daytime and rats through the night,
Rats on the platters and rats on the tiles,
Rat claws that clatter and rats fat and vile.

And it wasn't just that they were plentiful. They were rude and saucy beyond belief, as if they knew that no one in Hamelin was smart or powerful enough to stop their relentless advance. They were like a triumphant army that invades a town, that takes over every store and granary and seizes every house to shelter its soldiers. They did as they pleased. They knew no fear. And then the Piper came. In a trice, the rats were gone.

Except in my dreams. In my dreams, rats would back me into corners, chew on my hair, shove me into closets and bar the door, creep across my feet or face, nuzzle my cheek and fill my ears with dark whisperings in their secret rat language. All night long I would live with the rats, fearful and alert. Then morning would come. The sun would shine. Ebba would gently shake me awake. I would rise and straighten my twisted bedclothes. I would sit down for breakfast knowing very well that the rats belonged to the past. Even so, my dreams stuck fast. They were so fresh in my memory that I would more than half believe I could see rats swimming in the basin, peering from the teapot. I was always on guard, in case one strolled casually across the table to snatch the egg right out of my cup and roll it away like a ball.

My name is Penelope, and even though I am 101, I can remember the dream I had on that particular night, all those years ago. On the night my ten years became eleven. I was in the Hamelin Town Hall. In my dream, I mean. Children were not welcome in those hallowed chambers, and I had never entered there before. Even so, I knew right away where I was, for dreaming brings you knowledge you do not own in the waking world.

Torches burned. The air was dim with soot and haze. In the middle of the room was a massive oak table, strewn with the remains of a feast. Rats scaled the table legs. They skipped along the surface, helping themselves to leftovers. Bread and cake crumbs. Morsels of meat. Parings of fruit and cheese.

Around the dreamtime table sat a group of seven men: six town councillors and the Mayor. The Mayor was resplendent in his robe of purple velvet and white ermine. His golden chain of office hung heavily about his neck. The councillors were troubled. Each one's brow was more furrowed than the next. They had been arguing. The Mayor smashed his gavel down on the table. The loud wallop scattered the rats. One made a beeline up the Mayor's robe and took refuge behind the brim of his fur cap. It peered over the edge, looking for all the world as if it were enjoying the view from an alpine peak. The Mayor hammered his gavel again, more forcefully this time. The jabbering ceased.

"Order! Gentlemen, come to order! Important business is at hand, as you well know. We can no longer brook delay in this most pressing matter. We must make a decision tonight about how we will bring the Plague to an end. The population of rats is growing by such leaps and bounds that Hamelin will soon be uninhabitable by human beings. Citizens talk of leaving. They say they will abandon their homes if something isn't done. Unless drastic means are taken to rid Hamelin of the Plague, we might just as well relinquish our keys to the rats themselves. Alderman Jambert, would you be kind enough to read out our draft of the resolution?"

The Jambert of my dream looked just like the Jambert I was accustomed to seeing around the town: a fleshy man with a beet-colored face and a nose that looked as if it had lost an angry argument with a wall. He unfurled a long scroll. A pair of rats tumbled from the parchment. They squeaked vengefully and bobbled off into dark corners. Jambert cleared his throat. The sound was like a dray horse pulling a loaded wagon over gravel. He read:

"We, the Mayor and Council of Hamelin, which fair town has been latterly troubled beyond all endurance by an infestation of rats, do hereby resolve to put an end to that pestilence once and for all. We record here that every usual and proven method of achieving this end has failed. An army of cats was deployed. They did valiant work, but still the rats multiplied. Thousands of traps were laid, each baited with fine cheese. The rats were not deterred. They sprang each trap without harm and waltzed away with cheddar on their breath. We have tried to block them out, burn them out, coax them out and cajole them out. We have tried to freeze them out, frighten them out, hound them out and harry them out, and still they multiply. As every sensible method has been found wanting, we have determined that we will essay the nonsensical."

"Nonsensical. That's putting it mildly," sputtered an alderman named Pirran.

"Quiet!" barked the Mayor. "You are out of order."

"Begging your pardon, Your Worship, but this whole notion is out of order, and I would be remiss if I didn't—"

But the Mayor silenced him with an angry growl. "Please continue, Alderman Jambert."

"Yes. Certainly. As I was saying, we have determined that we will essay the nonsensical. We have received a proposal from a piper who claims to play so sweetly that he will capture the rats in a net of music . . ."

"Preposterous!" hissed Pirran. The Mayor threatened him with his gavel.

". . . he will capture the rats in a net of music and lead them out of Hamelin. He promises that, for a fee of five hundred gold pieces, we shall never see them again."

"I still say it's piracy!" exploded Pirran.

How they resolved their differences I never knew. For, as the dreamtime council chamber exploded with shouts and accusations, I flew straight up through the roof, which was made of nothing thicker than clouds. High, high above Hamelin I floated. I could see for miles around. The fields of flax that surround the town. The hills beyond them, and the tall black mountains beyond the hills. But the laneways and roads were obscured by a turbulent brown current. It shuddered and seethed. It heaved and hummed. The streets of Hamelin had become a vibrating river of rats. How many? No one could count them. No one could name a number high enough. It was impossible to tell where one rat ended and the next one began. Tens of thousands of tails, hundreds of thousands of feet, millions of whiskers merged as the hastening tide cascaded past the school and the shops, the houses and the hall.

What an extraordinary noise! The hurried patter of so many feet made a rumble like the earth coming slowly unseamed. Riding above it all, high and lilting, was the trill of a pipe. Sweet. Fast. Alluring. As if every possible sound and mood were folded into one. The rats tried to caper and dance, but they were wedged so tightly that they could only move forward in tight circles, like little whirlpools.

I hung in the air and watched the rats flood out of Hamelin. They churned over the hills. They were swallowed by the distance. And then there was silence. When I looked down, I saw that I was hovering above our house. Somehow, I was able to see through the roof. I saw my mother and father sitting at the kitchen table. I saw Sophy, making her baskets. I saw Alloway, playing his harp. And I saw myself, Penelope, asleep on my bed. I called out to them, but the other Penelope was the only one to register my voice. I saw her open her eyes.

They locked with mine, and she willed me to come down. She pulled me towards her as if I were a trout on an invisible line. I entered my own flesh. I opened my own eyes. The dreaming was done, and my new life was about to begin.

7

The first to wake

Sleeping late should be a birthday morning privilege, but on the day I stopped being ten, I was the first in our house to wake. Scally had positioned himself over my nose and mouth like a furry mask. I sat bolt upright and sent him flying. He landed at the foot of the bed, wearing his own mask of half surprise, half disdain. As he gathered up his dignity he stared at me with his amazing eyes, which shifted readily from yellow to green. Then he blinked, raised a paw as though in mock salute, and applied himself to licking it deeply.

Scally was not a cat who suffered insults gladly or in silence. It is almost certain that he also hissed or yowled. I can't say for sure, because by the time I woke, my ears had been stopped up for good and forever. If I failed at first to notice my new deafness, it was because my head still rang with the voices of my dreams. The raucous crowing of the aldermen. The rolling rumble of the rats. And most particularly, the high lilt of the Piper's flute. I lay back on my pillows and turned over in my mind the dream events I had just witnessed. As I saw them again on the back of my closed eyes, I remembered the day the Piper came to deliver us from the Plague.

It was April 8, exactly three months before my birthday. Early that morning, Grimbald, the beadle, had made his way through the streets. He knocked on every door. At every house he delivered the same message. As always, he spoke in verse, which in those days was a requirement of the job.

"Assembly today in the market square! No exceptions! You must be there! Don't come late! Get ready soon! The mayor will speak at precisely noon!"

"Ho, Grimbald," called Govan when the beadle came to our house. "What's this all about, then?"

"No time to chat! I have to run! I have to talk to everyone! The only thing I'll say is that it has to do with rats, rats, rats!"

"Not again!" Govan said to Ebba. "What pea-brained plan have they come up with this time?"

The people of Hamelin had often been summoned to the square to hear about some new scheme to rid the town of its rats. Each one was more unlikely or desperate than the last. So it was a restive group of citizens who gathered on that April day at noon when, once again, the Council stood before us.

"Citizens and friends!" declaimed the Mayor. "Today, at last, we bid farewell to the rats."

But the townsfolk had reached their limit. The crowd began to boo and whistle. The councillors shifted nervously on their feet. The Mayor raised his hands to signal for quiet.

"Today, we have engaged the services of a piper of great renown. A piper who plays music so sweet that he will capture the rats in a net of music."

Again the assembly erupted into jeers and jibes. The Mayor's forehead was dotted with sweat.

"Citizens and friends," he bellowed above the catcalls, "I present to you—our savior!"

The Mayor stood aside, and there stepped forward a most unusual man. He was dressed in a threadbare cloak of vivid green and yellow patchwork. He wore a matching tunic, and a cap of the same piebald fabric pulled low on his brow. His face was long and bony and jagged. A thin scraggle of beard hung from his chin. His eyes, just visible below the cap's brim, were hollow and bright. He was specter thin, all height and no width. He had so little substance he might as well have been transparent.

"Good people of Hamelin, I present to you the Pied Piper. He has come to deliver us from the Plague."

By now, the crowd was hooting and stamping and ready for blood. "Hey, Piper!" someone shouted. "Deliver us from the Mayor first!"

"String them both up!" cried someone else.

The Mayor cupped his hands to his mouth. "And now, let the piping begin!"

In his right hand, the Piper held a small flute. It was made from a reed such as you might find growing by the side of the road in a marsh. The idea that this strange man could rid the town of the pestilence by tootling on so small a pipe was simply too absurd to credit. Someone threw a bottle. Someone threw a boot. Someone began chanting, "Hang them all! Hang them all!" The Mayor and his men began to edge back. The crowd began to inch forward. The Piper raised his hand. He was such an arresting figure that the mob stopped in its tracks. An uneasy silence fell. He said nothing. He put his flute to his lips.

That was a day I will never forget. That was the day I remembered three months later, on the morning of my eleventh birthday. I lay in bed, recalling the way the Piper had raised his flute and blown. He blew, but no sound came forth. The throng began again to move menacingly towards the platform. But the rush of a sudden current between our ankles made everyone look down. What we saw beggared belief. Rats were on the move. The noontime streets were alive with their running. They dropped from their hiding places like ripe fruit. They fell from the roofs and the eaves. They tumbled from the steeples and the trees. Mesmerized by a music none of us could hear, they hit the ground dancing. In their hundreds, in their thousands, in their tens of thousands they followed the Piper as he walked quickly and deliberately out of town. Our angry desperation turned to joyful celebration. Cheers swallowed jeers. We whistled and clapped and roared. Hats and babies were thrown in the air. No one had ever known a happier day or a more uncommon parade. The rats followed the Piper out of Hamelin as he blew and blew on that little flute, and never did we hear his persuasive tune.

In my dream I had heard it, though. In my dream of flying, I had heard that powerful melody. On the morning of my birthday I lay in bed, and stroked Scally, and tried to remember the lilt of it. I was so absorbed by this that I didn't notice Ebba enter the room, didn't know she was there until she was shaking me. I turned to her. I saw the alarm on her face. I saw her lips move. But there was no sound. There would never be a sound again.

Section II

The Piper Returns

8

A Patchwork Legend

The old like to give advice to the young, but the young do not care to receive it. This is the way of the world. When I became an old lady—and I have been an old lady for a very long time—I promised myself that I would not give in to that temptation. I am pleased to say I have almost always kept my promise. Sometimes, I have had to bite my tongue. Sometimes, to be sure, I should have bitten it harder. Mostly, though, I have left to others the usual admonitions. Look before you leap. Think before you speak. Walk before you run.

When you are young, it is tiresome to hear reminders of such simple rules. But it is precisely because they are simple that we so often ignore them. There is no quicker route to trouble than overlooking the simple rules. Ah, well. Everyone learns this in his or her own way. The lucky ones come out of trouble both wiser and unharmed. For the lucky ones, trouble can be a great teacher.

I say I have made it a rule not to preach. However, anyone who is 101 has earned the right to break her own rules. Once in a while, at least. And so, I am going to give you one piece of advice. Pause once a day and relish the moment. Look around. Notice the colors, the smells and the sounds. Take them in, for that moment will pass and no one can say what the next moment will bring.

I know this better than most. One moment I heard. The next moment I didn't. There was no warning. I woke, and an important way of knowing the world was gone from me.

In all my 101 years I have never known a day as frightening or as eventful as the day of my eleventh birthday. I say this with certainty, although in truth I recall almost nothing of it. The terrible surprise of my sudden deafness, and the even worse shock of what the afternoon would bring, robbed me of my memory. It was as if that day was so dark that my mind folded in on itself, protectively, the way a daisy will at night. The story of that day is a story I know well. It is a story I have often told. But it is a story I have learned secondhand. I learned it in a patchwork way, over the years that followed, from Ebba and Govan, from Alloway and Sophy. I learned the story of that day as though it were a legend. Which, in a way, it is.

Ebba's story

I meant to make you waffles. I knew how much you liked them. They were always your favorite, waffles were, and I wanted to surprise you for your birthday breakfast. I intended to get an early start, because you know how fussy they can be to fix. The first few always stick to the griddle. I didn't want to wake your father, so I moved about our room on tiptoe. Even so, he opened his eyes. He used to sleep so soundly, but his illness changed all that.

"What are you doing?" he asked, and I told him what I was about. He smiled and sang a little song that popped into his head.

Penelope sweet, your birthday treat
Is something that you love to eat.

Tasty morsels, nothing awful,
Rise and shine and come for waffles.

"Clever Govan," I said.

"Ebba, Ebba. If only I could be half as clever as you. What would the world be worse off without? Waffles? Or a stiff old man's silly songs?"

"Hush," I said, for it pained me to see him so discouraged. "It's a lovely song. Penelope will be thrilled. Try to get some more sleep."

In truth, it was a silly ditty, but the melody was catchy. I hummed it as I walked down the hallway to the kitchen. I passed your room and decided to look in on you. I was sure you'd still be dead to the world. You always did love to sleep in. But no. I opened the door a crack and saw that you were wide awake. You were lying in bed with Scally on your chest. You had a faraway look in your eyes. I thought you were lost in a daydream. It wouldn't have been the first time. I must have stood there for a full minute. I smiled, thinking of how soon you would be a woman. In just a few hours you would put on the new white robe I had stitched for you, and we would make our way to Cuthbert's hut. How curious I was to find out what he would tell you.

Govan's song was still circling in my head. I knew how pleased you'd be to hear it. I opened the door full wide. Scally looked my way, out of the corner of an eye, but you never turned your head. I cleared my throat and sang. Still, you looked straight ahead. I wondered if you might be mocking me, pretending to ignore me in that way, but it was so unlike you. I was sure something was wrong. But what? All I could think to do was to sing again. Three times I sang that nonsensical song. Each time I sang it louder than before.

Penelope sweet, your birthday treat
Is something that you love to eat.
Tasty morsels, nothing awful,
Rise and shine and come for waffles.

By the third time through, my heart had crept into my throat. You showed no sign of knowing I was there. I moved across the room. I crouched by your bed. I took you by your shoulders and shook you, harder than I'd intended. How strange that felt, for I had never laid a hand on either of my children in anger. Even so, I shook you and I shouted. "Rise and shine! Rise and shine! Rise and shine!" I hardly knew my own voice, it was so changed, so disguised by panic. Scally was enough alarmed he ran under the bed. You turned to me. "Mother?" You said the word, but never heard it. I read the confusion on your face. It was as if you were trying to decide if you were still asleep and dreaming. Then I heard my own voice exploding into the morning air. "Govan! Govan! Govan!" I folded you into my arms. In an instant came the hurried thud, thud, thud of his cane in the hall.

sophy's story

In the weeks before you turned eleven, I grew a little jealous. I'm not proud to say so. In my head, I knew it was ridiculous. Even so, in my heart I felt envy. I chided myself for it. I said,

"Sophy, you know very well that this happens to a girl only once in her lifetime. You know very well that your day has come and gone. Now, it is Penelope's turn. You must wish her well." And I did, little sister. Of course I did. For you I wanted all the happiness in the world. I told you so the day before everything changed. Do you remember? We sat together in the garden. We were shelling peas. You said, "Tell me again about your visit to Cuthbert."

"How many times have you heard that story?"

"A thousand."

"At least."

"It doesn't matter. Tell me again."

"You know it so well. And anyway, after tomorrow you'll have your own story to tell. It will be the happiest day of your life."

"I know. But tell me again."

And so I did. I told you what you already knew. I told you what had happened to me, which was exactly what had happened to every other girl in Hamelin for as long as anyone can remember. I told you about how at eleven o'clock on the morning of my eleventh birthday, Ebba and I left the house. As is the custom, I wore a long white robe and a garland of white flowers around my head. I remember that I gathered the robe up as we walked and held it off the ground, so as not to dirty the hem. It had rained the day before, and the roads were mucky. As is the custom, all the women in Hamelin came out to greet us. Some leaned down from their windows to smile and wave. Some stood in doorways holding their babies. Some gave me small good-luck gifts, coins and amulets. Charms for a safe passage. They pressed them into my hands and said, "Welcome, sister. Welcome." By which they meant that I was leaving the world of girlhood behind. I was becoming a woman. I remember how Ludmilla, the baker, teased me as we passed. "You watch out for that Cuthbert, Sophy. A pretty young thing like you, he might just decide to keep you for himself."

"Hush, Ludmilla," laughed Mother. "Cuthbert is far too old to have such thoughts. Why, he's a thousand if he's a day!"

"He's old, but I've heard tell that he's yeasty."

"Oh, Ludmilla! Go back to your scones. Pay no attention to her, Sophy," Mother said. Not that I minded Ludmilla teasing, or took her seriously. Somehow, I knew that my talents didn't include housekeeping for hermits. About my particular talent there was never any question. Mine had always been obvious. I sang before I talked. There was nothing to it. Singing simply lived in my throat. It was completely at home there, like a bird in a nest. Even as we left Hamelin and entered the forest, even as we followed the path that led to Cuthbert's hut, even before we saw the smoke from his chimney or heard Ulysses bark out the news of our arrival, I knew what would happen. Cuthbert would spread out his cards. He would look in his crystal. He would study my hand. He would look deep into my eyes. And he would tell us what we already knew. It would be no more difficult for him to see that than it would be to look at a face covered with red spots and say, "Measles."

If I was jealous, Penelope, this was why. Your talent had not yet made itself known. For you, there would be the pleasure of surprise. It is often said that the greatest gifts are the slowest to reveal themselves. You would return from Cuthbert's hut, and you would know something about yourself that none of us could ever have guessed or imagined. But nothing turned out as it ought to have done. In the end, the rarest of things happened. In the end, it was Cuthbert who came to you. It was I who went to fetch him. Ebba sent me.

"And hurry, Sophy. Something is dreadfully wrong with Penelope. Perhaps Cuthbert will know of some herb that will help. Perhaps he will have a charm."

"But Cuthbert never leaves the forest."

"On this one occasion, he will have to. He must. He is the only one who can help. Penelope cannot go to him. Hurry! Hurry!"

The steeple clock was chiming ten as I ran over the cobbles and across the square and down the streets and through the town gates.

"Ho, there, Sophy," called out Ludmilla. "Where's that sister of yours? Isn't it almost time for her to take the walk?" But I didn't even wave by way of acknowledgment. My heart raced apace with my feet as I pelted down the forest pathway, out of the sun and into the dappled shade. The fast beat inside my chest echoed in my head. "Cuth-bert, Cuth-bert, Cuth-bert." That was what it seemed to repeat. Every time it sang his name, I worried. I had never heard of him budging from his hut. Why would he come with me? How could I convince him that he must? What could I tell him to persuade him to pick up his stick and follow me home? "Cuth-bert, Cuth-bert, Cuth-bert." My breathing was ragged by the time I smelled the wood smoke from his fire and heard Ulysses start to bay.

It was as if the barking of the dog heralded the music. The

notes seemed to rise up from the ground and well out of the trees. They fell from the sky. They covered me, caught me like a wren in a net. I was taken mid-stride. I stood stock-still. I was frozen on the spot for what was probably a second or two but seemed an eternity. The strange, unearthly music washed over me in waves, high and sweet and dangerous. It thawed me. Motion returned, but not of my own will or making. I began to dance. I couldn't stop myself. My limbs jerked and angled this way and that. I was a windmill come unhinged in a lusty gale. I was a crazy marionette, and my strings were pulled by an even crazier puppeteer. The dance quickened to a whirl. I spun so fast I couldn't tell where my body ended and the music began. I felt as though my arms had traded place with my legs, as if my feet were where my head belonged. I was nothing but vibration. Then blackness took over.

How long I lingered in the dark I cannot say. I only know that when I woke again, all the happy past had ended with a shudder. All the horrible future had only just begun.

Govan's story

"I did not like that man." That's what I said to your mother one night, not long after the rats were gone, and everyone was singing the praises of the Piper.

"How can you like or dislike someone you don't know?"

"There was something about his eyes."

"I remember that they were bright."

"Bright, but empty."

"I can't say that I noticed, Govan. He rid us of the rats. For that I bless him."

"He rid us of the rats, but I still have an uneasy feeling about him."

"Govan, Govan. Not every silver lining has to have a cloud, you know."

The Piper so unnerved me that I wanted only to put him from my mind. Try as I might, he continued to occupy my thoughts. He was never more present than on the afternoon Alloway returned from the square. He had taken his harp to the market to play for coins. It is amazing how many people assume that because Alloway is blind he is stupid. It is amazing how often people will have private conversations within his easy earshot.

"Govan," he said, when he joined me by the hearth, "what would you say if I told you that our Mayor does not keep his word?"

"Alloway, nothing could surprise me less. I have never found our Mayor to be a very honorable man. Why do you ask such a question?"

"I overheard him and Alderman Pirran in the market just now. They were talking with the Piper."

Alloway said "Piper" and my spine ran chill.

"And what were they saying, our fine town fathers and the Piper?"

"The Piper was asking them for money. His fee for piping away the rats. 'Five hundred gold pieces, gentlemen. That was the price upon which we agreed, was it not?' "

Alloway, as you know, is a wicked mimic. I had not heard the Piper's voice before, and I was not glad to hear it then, coming from the mouth of my apprentice. It was sharp and purposeful. It was the voice of someone who was no stranger to cunning.

"By all means!" Alloway continued, speaking now in the voice of the Mayor. "But surely you understand that we don't keep such a hefty sum on hand. We must make arrangements with the treasury. But you will have your payment, just as we promised."

"I trust that I shall find it so. I will give you three more days. If you do not honor your promise by then, I shall have to take action."

Alloway reverted to his own voice.

"And he stalked away. I felt the breeze from his cloak as he strode by. The Mayor and Pirran waited till he was gone. Then the Mayor guffawed. 'Ha! It is to laugh, Pirran. It is to laugh. He'll never see his five hundred gold pieces.' "

"But he says he'll take action."

"Action? Let him try. We have the finest lawyers in the land. If he wants action, we'll show him action. He won't know what hit him."

"Nevertheless, he has a point, Your Wartship."

"Worship!"

"Yes, yes. Exactly what I meant to say, Your Worship. But the Piper has a point. He did as he promised. I always thought that five hundred gold pieces was outright robbery. I said so very plainly, if you'll recollect. But even so, a bargain is a bargain. Should we not pay him something?"

"Oh, very well, then. Why not send him a nice thank-you note, a box of chocolates and a bottle of port?"

"A bottle of port?"

"Come, come, Pirran. Surely you have such a thing in that cellar of yours. And perhaps we could include a portrait of me, as well. I believe there's a whole warehouse full of them. That's quite generous, don't you think? That should satisfy him. Five hundred gold pieces! Ha! The very idea!"

It is myself, Govan, I blame for what happened to Hamelin next. I ought to have seen it coming. I ought to have raised the alarm. I ought to have gone to the people myself and denounced the Mayor as a cheat and a liar. They would have listened if I'd put it in a song. But no. I mulled in silence. The three days passed. Your birthday came. And that was the day the Piper showed that he, at least, was a man of his word. It was on your birthday that the Piper returned to keep the promise he made to the Mayor. He came. He played. And by the time he stopped his piping, the only sound you could hear in Hamelin was mothers howling and fathers gnashing their teeth.

Alloway's story

Do you remember, Penelope, when I first came to stay? Govan was still full of vim, then, still loose of limb. His fingers held magic. With his harp he could conjure fire or ice. He could call up the sun or bring down the rain. He could play like the wind. He would sit at the harp, and you and Sophy would dance.

"Come, Alloway," you would say. "Dance with us."

But I never would.

"Come, Alloway! We'll teach you the steps. Don't be an old stick in the mud."

But I shook my head. I thought you wanted the fun of seeing me fall down or crash into the chairs and tables. At the orphanage there were those who enjoyed such cruel sport. But after some time had passed, I understood that you meant your invitation kindly. And the music was infectious. It had a way of getting to my feet. Before long, it had worked its way up my whole body. I began to sway in time in spite of myself.

"That's it, Alloway," you would call, "that's the way it starts. Now, come and dance."

And finally, after some more time had passed, I gave myself over to the melody and rhythm. I let myself dance. Do you remember, Penelope? They were short and halting steps at first. But before long, I was a madcap jigger. I would dance with you and Sophy, and then I'd take a solo turn. Ebba would clap and Govan played and sang. Slowly it settled on me that I had found my home. I had found my family. Alloway, the blind orphan no one wanted. Alloway, whose life began with abandonment. Alloway had found his place in the world. Alone in my room at night, I cried with the happiness of it. The scales that block my eyes should have been moved by those floods.

Even after Govan lost his music to the stiffness, and even after hard times settled on the house, I never worried that I might be sent away. I did what I could to help out. I took my harp to the market. I played for whatever coins or scraps came my way. To be sure, no one hearing me would mistake me for Govan, but I got by. I made friends among the stall keepers and merchants. They did what they could to help out. Ludmilla would sometimes send me home with a crusty loaf. Breenan, the butcher, would give me a chop for our supper. Hybald, the fruit seller, was generous with his oranges.

Sometimes, at night, I would play so that you and Sophy could dance. That always made me glad, although I often wished I could set down the harp and caper along for a round or two. Mind you, I did dance sometimes, when I was alone. I would turn and spin to whatever music happened to be in my head. Ebba caught me at it once. I don't know how long she might have watched me. I only know she didn't laugh. For that I bless her name, for surely I must have looked foolish.

"If I had to guess," she said, "I would say that you're dancing to 'The Harper Meets the Devil.' "

And she was exactly right. That was the very tune that was on my mind. It was among the first Govan had taught me. After that, her guessing became a private game between us. I would dance a jig or reel, and she would try to name the tune only I could hear. "Snow That Falls on Sunday" or "Jam Stains on the Linen" or "Kitten up the Maypole." It was Ebba who first saw me begin to dance on the day the Piper paid his final visit. Then, she was not so kindly.

"Alloway! This is no time for games! Stop it! Stop it!"

But stopping was not possible. I was obedient only to the swelling music that neither she nor Govan nor you, Penelope, could hear.

"Stop it, Alloway! For mercy's sake, stop it!"

But there was nothing to be done. Ebba's protests were lost in the sweet, swelling music. In seconds, everything I'd ever known was gone from me. All I owned was the giddy need to gallop. And that is what I did. Sightless and powerless, I galloped out into the world. And in the end, Penelope, it was I who finally brought you Cuthbert.

9

cuthbert comes

If you live to be 101, as I, Penelope, have done, you will find that everyone you meet asks the same impertinent questions. I have thought of wearing a plaque inscribed with the three most common inquiries, along with their answers.

> Q: Did you ever imagine you would live to be 101?
> A: Who could imagine something as absurd as living to be 101?
> Q: How does it feel to be 101?
> A: Much like being 99, only two years more brittle.
> Q: What is the best thing about being 101?
> A: Being absolutely certain of what you like. My favorite color is periwinkle. My favorite season is autumn. I prefer Thursday over all the other days of the week. I like dogs and cats equally. And my best friend is sleep.

I have always loved periwinkle and I have always loved sleep. When I was born, Ebba told me, the first thing I did, after letting go of a loud squawk, was to take a long snooze. Govan said no baby ever loved lullabies as much as I. And while Sophy would protest against her afternoon naps, I begged for them. Sleep was always there, as soon as I closed my eyes, carrying his big bag full of dreams.

Perhaps it is because of sleep that I have lived to this great age. Sleep has been more than my friend. He has been my healer. Whenever I have felt sad or distressed, he has hurried to help. When terrible things happen, I only have to close my eyes to make them go away. And when I wake, somehow, nothing seems as bad as it was. It's as if the world has become a softer place. As if an ointment has been spread on whatever wound was causing me pain.

Sleep did not desert me on the day I turned eleven, the very day the Piper returned to collect the debt he was owed. When the five hundred gold pieces he had been promised were not forthcoming, he took the children of Hamelin instead. He piped them away, just as easily as he had the rats. All the while the streets were full of the children's frenzied jumping and turning, sleep was nursing me through the first shock of deafness. All the while I slept, the parents of Hamelin howled their misery.

"As if the devil possessed her!" cried Newlyn the candle maker after she watched nine-year-old Petronilla scoop her baby brother, Basil, out of his cradle and whirl down the street.

"One like a crazy top! One like a mad dervish! I chased after them but could not keep up," wept Malo the tailor after his twin sons, Ouen and Oswin, spun out of his shop and down the road.

"I grabbed hold of her. I tried to keep her back. But she was too strong for me. She shook me off, brushed me away as though I were a tick. A little thing like that! Can you imagine?" said Frithbert the blacksmith. He was badly bruised after four-year-old Stithian fought clear of his arms to dance away behind the Piper.

Gildas, Juliana, Ogilvie and Ludhard. Wulfram, Wen, Tudwal and Alnoth. Campion, Senan, Blaise and Amphibalus. Pantaleon, Praxedes, Pandonia and Plunket. Children of the rich, and children of the poor. Children who had played ball, and tag, who had squabbled with their friends and been rude to their parents. Children who never ate their vegetables. Children who always said their prayers. Children I had known all my life. Children like Ives, who was thirteen, and who so surprised me during a game of hide and seek I gave him a black eye. Children like Dwyn, who was younger than I by just one day and with whom I had shared the excitement of turning eleven. One minute, the streets had been vibrant with the sounds of their games, their quarrels, their laughter. The next, there was nothing but the sound of their parents weeping.

What happened? What happened? Our poor little babies! Our sweet wee lambs! Such evil! Such evil! So terrible a man!

All of this I learned much later, of course. I had been eleven for two whole days before sleep returned me to a world where everything had changed. The first thing I saw when I opened my eyes was Scally. His back was arched. His hair stood on end. His mouth was drawn back in what I recognized as a hiss. I felt a damp tongue on my hand, and I looked down at the cause of the cat's alarm. It was a tall, lean black dog with worried eyes and a small stump where its right front leg ought to have been. And seated on a stool beside the dog, with quill in hand, inscribing words on a scroll of parchment, was an old man. His tunic was made of leather and so, it seemed, was his face. It was tanned and deeply lined, like a fresh-plowed field. He was as bald as the moon, but with magnificent eyebrows, like two great centipedes on his high forehead. And beneath those brows, he had such deep and kindly eyes. You had only to look into those eyes to know that there was no end to the pictures they contained. It was easy to imagine that they could see through any wall and over any distance. I had never seen such eyes before, had never seen the man who owned them. Even so, I knew his name as well as I knew my own. I knew it in my heart. Cuth-bert. Cuth-bert. He took me into his eyes. He sent me a long, slow wink. He smiled a long, slow smile. He dotted an "i". He crossed a "t". He finished his writing.

10

what cuthbert wrote

Dear Penelope,

Happy birthday and congratulations. Every girl should have a memorable elevening. I daresay yours has been one none of us will ever forget.

I wish it were possible for you to hear this. Luckily, Govan and Ebba say that you are adept both at reading and writing. You must always be grateful to them for giving you that gift of words. There are plenty who believe such learning belongs only to boys. It saddens me. Those who deny others knowledge do so because they live in fear. What are they afraid of? Of change, mostly. And of losing power. Such foolishness! Now they have seen how quickly change can come. Now they understand how little power they ever held. For in the end, there was nothing they could do to stop their own children.

They were powerless to hold back the flesh of their flesh when the Piper played his tune.

But wait. This will mean nothing to you yet. I tell my tale by chasing my tail. I am an old man. Rambling is my bad habit. I am Cuthbert, as you may have guessed. And the creature who has been trying to kiss you awake is no handsome prince. He is my old dog, Ulysses. You have slept a very long time, Penelope. You know nothing of these last two days. Even we who were awake and watching can hardly make sense of it. For now, it is enough to say that the Hamelin you knew is no more. You shall know the why and the how of it soon enough. Tomorrow, you may ask me as many questions as you wish. I will do my best to answer them.

I will tell you now, for you ought to know, that your deafness is nothing I can heal. There is no salve made of comfrey or lavender, no poultice of juniper or hyssop to coax sound back into your world. You are deaf, Penelope. You will want to weep over what you have lost. Weep you may and weep you must. But know this, as well, for whatever comfort it might bring you. Nothing happens without a reason, and sometimes our blessings come wearing grotesque disguises.

For now, drink what I give you. This infusion will help you sleep still more. Still more sleep is what you need, Penelope. You will wake in the morning with a clear mind. Until then, I will sit by your side. Sleep, Penelope. I will be here when you wake.

11

The Elevening Scrolls

Ninety years ago. Mercy! How can it be that ninety years have come and gone since Cuthbert turned up at our door? In spite of what my white hair and my stiff limbs tell me, I can hardly believe it's so. One thing I've learned in my 101 years is that Time is no liar. Time is honest. You can always depend on Time to be there, whether you want him to be or not. Time cannot be stopped or fooled. However, I have also learned that you can hold Time at bay by writing. Write something down and not even Time can take it away. For as long as you live on the earth, it will never be lost to you.

My proof for this is the "Elevening Scrolls." That is what I call the bundle of letters Cuthbert wrote to me in the days after I woke without my hearing. Inscribed upon the Elevening Scrolls are the words he chose to comfort me, as well as his answers to my questions. My many, many questions. For ninety years I have guarded these old parchments. I have kept them in a trunk, tightly rolled and tied with a ribbon. I fetched them down from the attic this morning. It has been a long, long time since I last studied them, but it took only one look for ninety years to melt away.

I remember so much of that day. The taste of the infusion—licorice and mint. The color of my room—periwinkle with buttermilk trim. The lapping of Ulysses' tongue—warm, wet velvet. And I remember how my head was full of a sound that was no sound at all. A low whooshing. A hollowness. As if I were hearing the rolling waves of a far-off sea.

Where are my parents?

"Asleep, just now. It has been days since they slept. You will see them soon."

What has happened?

"Great sadness. Great evil. Hamelin has lost its children."

How?

"The Piper has taken them. For want of five hundred gold pieces, he took them. Just as he took the rats. Just as he freed Hamelin of its pestilence, so he has robbed it of its joy."

The children? All of them?

"All but two."

And I am one?

"Yes."

Sophy?

"Gone."

Gone where?

"Gone with the Piper. Caught in his net of music and dragged away like flounders, helpless and flapping. Other than that, I cannot say."

Alloway?

"Alloway is the other who was spared. He was infected by dancing, but his blindness saved him, as surely as your deafness saved you. You could not hear the Piper's tune, and Alloway could not see to follow. It was Ulysses who found him, deep in the forest. Lost. Bruised. Exhausted. Ulysses led him to me. And Alloway brought me to you."

Where is he?

"You will see him before long. Like Ebba and Govan, he

sleeps. Ulysses guards him. Only we two are awake."

I wish I were asleep, too. If only this could be a dream!

And then I remember that I wept. I cried great, heaving sobs. I cried for everything I'd had and everything that was lost. Cuthbert wiped my tears with the soft sleeve of his tunic.

"Cry as much as you need," he wrote. "Crying soothes. It is true that your day of elevening is gone. Nothing can replace that. But you will know about your gifts, and soon enough. When Govan and Ebba and Alloway come back to the world, I will tell what I have to tell. But now, Penelope, it is my stomach that talks loudest. I believe it is asking for bacon and eggs. Will you join my stomach and me for some breakfast?"

I looked into Cuthbert's deep eyes and saw a golden light dancing there. I felt my mouth tug up at its corners. Cuthbert smiled back. For the first time in days, I put my feet on the floor. I stood on shaky legs. I followed Cuthbert through the brand-new world. Everything had changed. Even so, the sun still rose and the sun still set. I could no longer hear the ticking of the kitchen clock, but Time was still present and Time was still passing. I couldn't hear the pop and hiss from the skillet, but there was still such a thing as bacon, and it could still be fried. And still it was good to eat.

12

A Strange Gift

"Dangerous."

That was the first word I ever lip-read, ninety years ago.

"Dangerous."

Three syllables with a soft center.

"Dangerous."

Not an easy word for a novice to recognize. Still, I saw its shape on Ebba's mouth. There was no mistaking it. She spoke it slowly and deliberately. And she pounded her fists on the table. They thudded down and made no noise. The teacups jumped from their saucers and landed without a rattle.

"No! I won't allow it! How could you suggest such a thing, Cuthbert? She is all we have left!"

We were five at the table. Govan. Ebba. Cuthbert. Alloway. Me. Alloway had hugged me so hard when he saw me that I wondered if he might squeeze the breath right out of me. He was marked by misadventure. His knees and shins were bruised. His face was badly scratched. Now and again, Ulysses would stand on his hind legs, put his one front paw on Alloway's shoulder, and lick at the wounds. Scally watched this nursing with haughty disdain. He curled himself in an "S" around my shoulders. I could feel his purring thrum against my neck.

"Govan! Say something!"

"Ebba, be calm. Dangerous, of course. But what choice do we have? What choice if we want to see Sophy again? Sophy and all the others? And if Penelope has been given such a gift, then perhaps it was for this very reason."

"Dangerous and impossible! You heard what he said. A journey she takes while she's asleep? A journey that's a dream and yet more than a dream? How can we agree to such a thing?"

"Ebba. There is much we don't understand."

"Exactly. How can Penelope be lying asleep in her bed, yet at the same time be gallivanting around looking for the Piper? And what if she finds him, Govan? What then?"

"Ebba has a point, Cuthbert. What assurance do we have that Penelope will return safely?"

"I offer no assurance, Govan. There are risks. It might *well* be dangerous."

There it was again. "Dangerous" was the only word I understood of this back and forth between my parents and Cuthbert. It was Alloway who later told me what they had said. Even in the absence of words, I could tell that the argument was heated and serious. And I knew that it had to do with me. I knew it had to do with my gift. It had been revealed to them. To me, it was still a mystery.

My gift! For so many years I had feared it would be ordinary. I had worried that, on the day of my elevening, Cuthbert would say, "Penelope's future is with goats and cabbages." Or, "Penelope has it in her to bake puffy scones and a very moist chocolate cake." Or, "If she is diligent, Penelope will one day knit a muffler that will keep her husband warm and happy."

How I dreaded it! But what else might there be for me, other than skipping? I had settled my mind to the certainty that my gift would be ordinary, and my future dull. I could never in a million years of guessing have imagined what Cuthbert would tell me. Here are his words from the Elevening Scrolls.

My dear Penelope:

Now is the day for which you have waited so long. Now, you shall learn about your gift. The words I will write are simple, but they carry on their backs ideas that are thorny and difficult to grasp. They might seem like nonsense to you at first. I can only assure you that when you have lived with them a while, you will come to understand them.

Nothing is accidental. Nothing happens by chance. The people we meet, the places we visit, the opportunities we are given: everything has a reason. This is also true of the misfortunes that befall us. Even the tragedies that are visited upon us are never without purpose, although it may take us many years to understand what such a purpose might be. Even the great sadness of your deafness has a reason behind it. Impossible though this may be to believe, it is, in its own way, a gift.

You may think me a madman to say such a thing. Deafness? A gift? Surely it is a curse. It is no more a blessing than if you had been given a ball and chain to haul along behind you, all the days of your life. I understand that this is what you must feel. It is only natural. But think for a minute of where you would be, had you not been robbed of your hearing on the morning of your elevening. You would be with the others. Wherever the others might be. Think of what you were spared, Penelope, because of your deafness. Because you were unable to hear the music that captured every other child, you escaped the Piper's snare. And while you might very well wonder why you were afflicted with deafness, you must also ask yourself, "Why was I saved? Why me, rather than some other child?"

Nothing is accidental. Nothing happens by chance. If you were passed over, it was for a reason. It is because you have important work to do. You have a mission. You have been singled out because you alone hold the power to find and save the children of Hamelin. And the source of that power, Penelope, is your gift.

It was ninety years ago that I first read those words. I remember how I looked up from the parchment. My gaze locked with Ebba's. Her eyes filled with tears. I was about to learn what she already knew. About to learn why she again raised her hand and then brought it down hard on the table. Again, I saw that word on her lips.

"Dangerous!"

13

A Strange Mission

It is nighttime now. The sky above Hamelin is a field thickly planted with stars. It is as black and clear a sky as I can ever remember. By morning, though, clouds will have gathered. By morning, we will have rain. I am never wrong about the rain. My scar gives it away every time. My scar is more reliable than any barometer. Whenever my scar starts first to tingle and then to throb, I know it won't be long until the thunder rolls.

My scar. It is a treasured souvenir. Whenever I pass a mirror, whenever Mellon and his vile confederates treat me to a chorus of "Harpy, Harpy Scarface," whenever I sense a change in the weather, my scar reminds me of my travels. Of the perilous voyage my gift made possible. Made necessary. A strange gift. A rare gift. The gift of Deep Dreaming.

And now I must tell you of it, but oh! My poor hand! How stiff it is! How sore! And little wonder. I have written all day. Now I know better how old Cuthbert must have felt, scribbling his answers to my many questions. I have them in front of me, on the tattered Elevening Scrolls. I will copy them out, then reward myself with a long, hot bath.

I don't understand, Cuthbert. How can dreaming be a gift? Everyone dreams!

"No, Penelope. Not dreaming. Look again."

I read aloud what he had written. I can still remember the feel of my tongue against my teeth, shaping his words. I can still remember how strange it was not to hear the sounds I knew I was making. *"Yours is a gift that is rarely bestowed. You have been given the gift called Deep Dreaming."*

"Deep Dreaming, Penelope. That is altogether different from the ordinary dreaming of ordinary people."

But how? Why? What does it mean?

"Be patient. You are like a baby who is born into a brand-new world and wants to understand it all in a single glance. It is not possible to explain Deep Dreaming as easily as one might tell how to nail a board or make an omelette. Let me begin with a question. What happens to the waking world when we fall asleep? When we leave it behind and begin to dream?"

Nothing at all, of course. It goes on and on.

"And how do you know?"

Because that is the way I find it. When I wake in the morning, the world is still as it was when I went to bed the night before. Nothing has changed. At least—until today.

"Very good. Now, tell me what happens to your dreams when you awake."

What happens? Why, they disappear.

"No. That is what most people believe, but it is not so. The world of dreaming does not end with waking any more than the world of waking ends with dreaming. Think of the stars. We see them by night. By day, they are invisible. Even so, we know they are there, pinned to the sky above us. We know that when darkness falls they will reveal themselves again. In the same way, dreams go on and on, even though we do not see them. Dreams are like another country, where everyone can travel a little. But for most people, the stay is brief. And most people forget what they saw there as soon as they open their eyes. It is only those who have the gift of Deep Dreaming who can do otherwise."

But I have always been able to remember my dreams.

"Deep Dreaming is more than mere remembering. Deep Dreaming is like having a passport to that other country. It is like having a key to the city. It gives you certain privileges. It allows you to linger longer than most. It allows you to cross borders."

Cross borders?

"For those who are very gifted, it is sometimes possible for the dream self to cross into the world of the waking."

How do you know all this?

"I am very old, Penelope. Very, very old. I know many things. Suffice it to say that I have been a dabbler in the world of Deep Dreaming. It is a territory that I once explored. When I was young."

You have this gift?

"Not in the same degree. Every talent, whether it is running or singing or painting or harp playing, is bestowed in different measure. As at a banquet, not everyone receives the same helping. My own bowl contained but a meager portion of Deep Dreaming."

Oh, Cuthbert. How can I take this in? My head is spinning.

"Of course it is spinning. For eleven years you have lived believing that black is black and white is white, and now you are told that this is not really so. For eleven years you have lived believing that what is real is the hard earth beneath your feet. Now you are told of a whole other world, a neighboring world, that is every bit as real, even though it is not made of anything solid. What could be more natural than that your head might spin at such news?"

Even if what you say is so, what good is such a gift? And what has it got to do with the Piper?

"It is what you and the Piper have in common. He is also a Deep Dreamer. His is a very great gift. He is one of the few who can cross the border between waking and sleeping. What's more, he has learned how to snare the waking, to abduct them and haul them after him into the country of his own dreaming. And that is where he has taken your sister, Penelope. That is where you will find Sophy and all the others. Only someone as powerful as the Piper can ever hope to bring them home."

Me?

"There is no one else."

What about you?

"I am too old. And my gift was small. It would never have

been strong enough to match his. Yours is, Penelope. You must merely use it."

But how?

"By knowing that you can. By believing. By giving yourself up to sleep. By entering your own dream. By willfully searching."

At this point, I remember I laughed. It was like being told I could flap my arms and fly to the moon. Surely it must all be a terrible joke. But Cuthbert's face was serious. Deadly serious, so I held my laughter in. *You say I must give myself up to sleep before I can search for them. Does this mean I will be in two places at once? Will I be here, asleep in my bed, and also there? In the world of dreaming?*

"In a way, yes. Flesh-and-blood Penelope will stay in this world. Dreamtime Penelope will travel to the other."

What if something happens to the dreamtime Penelope?

"That is the hardest question of all."

I could die?

"I cannot say."

I could sleep forever?

"Penelope, Penelope! These are questions anyone would ask, and yet they are questions I cannot answer. Try not to cloud your mind with them."

How long will I sleep?

"As long as is needed to complete the dreaming."

A minute? An hour?

"Perhaps one. Perhaps the other. Time, like everything else, is different in that country. It isn't measured in minutes and hours."

And I must go alone?

"You must start out alone. You will find companions along the way."

I am frightened.

"Of course you are. But you must remember: gifts such as yours are not given to those who are unable to use them. You must have confidence, Penelope. And although I am too old to come with you, I am not without my powers. I will find a way to follow your path from the world of the waking. I will find a way to bring you word. I will come to you three times, Penelope. Look for me in glass."

Glass?

"You will understand soon. If you go. Will you go, Penelope?"

Yes. Yes, I will go. Tonight, Cuthbert. I will go.

14

Letters and charms

I will go. With those three words I sealed my fate and settled my future. I took my first step along the path to where I have arrived. To what I have become. An old woman, bent and proud and scorned. Harpy, Harpy Scarface.

I was nervous as I lay under my quilt. Ebba, Govan, Alloway and Cuthbert were gathered about my bed. Three-legged Ulysses was there, too. Scally jumped up and curled himself on my chest.

I still have that bed. Ninety years later, it is still the place I lay my head. And I still have the letters I was given on that long-ago night. The wishes for safe passage. I have kept them bundled up with the Elevening Scrolls. Here is Alloway's short note, written out in Ebba's hand:

Dear Penelope:

Cuthbert says that in your world of Deep Dreaming, perhaps you will be able to hear. Could I see there, I wonder? I wish I could go with you and find out. But you must go on your own.

I have made you a good-bye gift, a necklace. I fear it may not be very pretty, but I have braided it from harp strings. Eight of them, all the notes in the scale. Govan played on these strings. So did I. There is music in this necklace, Penelope. It is for you to wear while you sleep. It is for you to carry with you, if you are able. It is to remind you of home and everyone who lives here. Good luck. Don't stay away too long. We will miss you.

I fastened his gift around my neck and read the next letter, also written in Ebba's hand.

Dear Daughter:

We love you and we love your sister. Have we said that often enough? Perhaps not. Still, we hope you know that it is so. For you and for Sophy we have always wanted nothing but happiness and light. That is every parent's wish for every child. It is a foolish wish, for it can never be granted. There will always be sadness. Somehow, somewhere, darkness will always fall.

But who could have imagined this? Your deafness. The Piper. The children. The world turned upside down.

You have made a dangerous choice. In the world we used to know, no parent would allow a child to venture into the unknown. But that world is gone, and so are its rules. Perhaps this is not a bad thing. In that world, the men in whom we put our trust sold our children for five hundred gold coins. They were liars and cheats. They held open the door to evil. They invited it in, and we have all reaped the consequences. The price we paid was our happiness.

And now you are determined to travel. It is far too heavy a weight to put on the back of a child, but there is no one else who can bear it. And so we give you our blessing. We wish you a safe voyage. Find your sister, Penelope. Find the others. Bring them home. We will wait for you. We love you. You are braver than we ever knew! And when you come back, you shall have waffles every day for a week.

Govan took my hand with his gnarled fingers, and Ebba leaned down and kissed me five times, just as she had done every night for as long as I could remember. Forehead, cheek, chin, cheek, forehead. Her magic circle to keep me from harm. Cuthbert too had a charm to offer. A charm for good dreaming.

I am Cuthbert the sage and the seer of gifts.
I am Cuthbert the sage and the speaker of charms.
I summon whatever the spirit that lifts
The wakeful to sleeping and keeps them from harm.

I summon the spirit that brings on good sleep,
The spirit of dreaming I call as your guide.
I wish you a dream that is guarded and deep
And loving companions to walk by your side.
Sleep now, Penelope. Sleep and sleep well.
Sleep now, Penelope. Sleep and sleep tight.
Dream now, Penelope. Dream dreams that tell
The way out of darkness and back to the light.

I looked around the room, seeing the sadness and anxiety on every face. I placed my hands one on each side of the purring cat. I could feel him throb. I took comfort from his warmth. It was time to go. I closed my eyes. I invited sleep in.

Section III

Deep Dreaming

15

Falling, and what came After

I felt the bed rise. Then it commenced to whirl. The faster it spun, the higher it rose. And when the spinning stopped, the bed disappeared altogether. I was no longer in our house, in my room. I was outside, suspended above some unknown landscape. I hung in midair, floating like a vapor.

I looked down, and who should I see? Me, Penelope. Only it wasn't precisely me. It was my dream self. The dreamtime Penelope was skipping rope, a running skip. She dashed pell-mell across a grassy field. The rope was a blur. She skipped fast as the wind. Fast as a dancing doe. She skipped so fast her feet scarcely grazed the ground. It was as if she were made of nothing but air and happiness.

Carefree she might have been, but she was careless, too. Hanging above her, I saw what she couldn't. I saw she was approaching the edge of a cliff. I tried to shout a warning, but no sound came. The earth began to give way beneath her feet. She skipped blissfully into nothingness.

Something told me to dive after her. I didn't hesitate. She had a head start, but somehow I caught up with her. I drew level with my double. She kept me in her orbit, like the earth holds the moon. Together we fell, two stones of equal weight, face to face. And still she was turning rope. She never stopped. She turned as if nothing were amiss. She turned and she chanted:

Fillery, follery, fickery, fin,
Now I call Penelope in!

I can tell you that it is peculiar to be invited to skip with yourself. But who could decline the invitation? Surely not me. I jumped to join her. The rope passed over my head. It passed beneath my feet; beneath hers, too. By the time the circle was complete, we two Penelopes had somehow absorbed each other. Now, only one Penelope was falling. Falling and falling. Down and down.

I had never made a study of cliffs. After all, we did not have many cliffs in the vicinity of Hamelin. However, I felt quite sure that a proper cliff was meant to eventually connect with the ground. This cliff did not obey the rule. This cliff seemed to have no bottom. Hours whizzed by, or seemed to. I wondered if for the rest of my life there would be no direction other than down. As there was nothing to do but fall, I passed the time by jumping rope.

Skipping in the darkness,
Skipping in the air.
Who knows where we're going
Till we land down there?

That was what I sang. Looking back, I am impressed at how calm I was, all things considered. I was curiously unafraid, even when I landed with a graceless thud. Rarely has a journey come to so abrupt an end. Limbs splayed, I lay winded on damp ground. All was dark. I saw nothing of where I was.

"Goose?"

A voice. Whose? Strange, yet not. Unknown, yet familiar.

"Are you alive?"

A good question. I moved my arms. They seemed to work. I lifted each leg. They obeyed my commands. I touched my throat. The necklace that Alloway had given me was still round my neck. And the skipping rope of the dreamtime Penelope lay at my side, curled on the ground like a snake. Gingerly, slowly, I sat upright. I leaned my back against a wall.

"Goose."

The voice echoed. The wall was stone and damp. A cave, then?

"Goose! Can you hear me?"

Hear? No, of course I couldn't hear. I was deaf. And yet—

"Goose! Answer me!"

The voice persisted. Was it perhaps just inside my head?

"Who are you?"

I formed the words with my lips. They fell from my mouth and entered my ears. They rang there, loud and clear. How I grinned. Even though I was in a strange place, in a strange world, in a dark cave, with an unseen stranger for company, I nearly split my face with smiling. I could hear! Wherever I was and however I had arrived, I had found the precious thing I'd lost. I was invaded by a shining joy. I had heard my own words. My own question. I asked it again.

"Who are you?"

"Who am I?"

The voice again, incredulous this time.

"Oh, Goose! After all these years! Don't you even know my voice?"

I peered around me. I surveyed the dark. I made out two beams of light. They moved through the air towards me, flashing green, then yellow.

"Don't you know me, Goose?"

I squeezed my eyes tight. I opened them. I looked again. I made out a geometry of features. Triangle ears. Oval eyes. Small round nose. Slowly, I reached out. Slowly, I touched whatever it was. It was a head. What's more, it was a head I knew. I ran my hand over whiskers and down the known path of a warm back. I felt an accustomed twitch of tail. It couldn't be! How was it possible?

"Scally?"

"None other, my darling Goose. None other. May I join you?"

And without waiting for an answer, my dear cat settled into my lap, rumbling with a rich and throaty purr of abiding contentment.

16

companions along the way

Our fat cat, Scallywaggle, was the same age as Sophy, almost to the day. He came to us as a tiny kitten just a few weeks after she was born. It was young Gregor, one of Govan's apprentices, who heard the cat's pathetic mewing and rescued him from a ditch. Gregor brought the foundling home. Ebba, tender-hearted as always, nursed him back to health. Scally survived. He prospered. He soon became part of the family. He was there when I was born. I had known him all my life.

My first memory is of Scally. I was still a baby, not yet two. I was lying in my trundle bed. It was the middle of the afternoon. Those were Plague years and rats were everywhere. I was too young to understand what they were. I had no name for the thing that crept across my quilt. It was a monster with a long, scaly tail. It was a demon with hot, red eyes.

I began to cry, a fretful wail. Where was Ebba? Where was Govan? Who could help me? Then came a calico blur. There was a sweep of paw, a snatch of jaw. There was a triumphant yowl. The rat was no more. I was safe. And on that day, a bond was forged between girl and cat.

From then on, Scally slept on my bed. He came to me when he wanted a tickle under the chin. He was patient with my games. He allowed me to dress him in a bonnet and didn't complain when I pressed him into service as a guest at pretend tea parties. The only game he resisted was "haircut." Sensibly, he would run away when he saw me coming with Ebba's shears.

I was Scally's favorite. I told him all my secrets. I confessed to him my fears, my small trespasses. I never once worried that he would give me away. I never once suspected that one day he would speak. Now, in this place so far from home, he lay in my lap. He purred like a conventional cat. I scooped him up and peered into the brilliant orbs of his eyes. They were all that was visible in the blackness.

"Not possible," I said.

"Why not?"

"Cats can't talk."

"Oh, but we can. We can, Goose! I have been talking to you your whole life long. I've told you where I've been. I've told you where I'm going. I've told you what I think, what I feel. I've told you of birds I have caught, of voles I have eaten. I have been telling you for the past six years that I prefer chicken to fish. I have asked you more often than I can think if you would scratch me behind my ears. In fact, could you oblige me now?"

"Which ear?"

"The right, please, dear heart. Lower. Higher. More to the left. Ah. Yes. Perfect."

He rumbled his pleasure.

"Yes, Goose. I have been talking to you since you drew your first breath. The problem has not been with my talking. It has been with your hearing. Mind, you are not alone. Most two-legs are the same."

"Two-legs?"

"I beg your pardon. That is what we call you humans. Very few of your kind have any notion that we cats have just as much to say as they do. In my opinion, our conversation is a great deal more interesting."

"So some humans can hear you?"

"A few. A very few. Cuthbert does."

"Cuthbert?"

"Yes. I can tell you, I gave him a piece of my mind when he brought that dog into the house."

"Ulysses."

"Ulysses or Aloysius or Sylvius or Thingamajig. I don't much care about his name. He is a nuisance, as are most dogs. All that panting. All that slavering. All that begging to be loved. Truly, Goose, they give me the willies."

He scrambled up to my shoulder.

"But why do you call me Goose?"

"Why? Because that is your name. Your cat name, that is."

"Pardon?"

"Your cat name. Parents bestow human names on their children. It was your mother and father who called you Penelope. It falls to cats to give out cat names. It was I who called you Goose."

"Why Goose?"

"You might just as well ask why Penelope. I called you Goose because it seemed to fit. You were plump. You squawked. You were forever eating. To me, you will always be Goose."

I felt for his chin and tickled him there. What did it all mean? Plainly, I had landed in a place where none of the old rules applied.

"What about cats, then? Do cats have names other than those we give them?"

"Of course. But there is no point in asking me mine. We are sworn to secrecy. If cats started blabbing their real names to all and sundry, who knows what might happen?"

Who knew what might happen? That was the question of the moment, and not just concerning the names of cats. We had a mission. We had a job to do. I was glad of Scally's company, and I was glad to see that Cuthbert had been right when he promised companions along the way.

"Scally, was it Cuthbert who sent you?"

"Oh, dearest Goose. I am a cat. I prize my independence above all else. No one sends me anywhere, not even the great Cuthbert."

"Then how did you get here? How did you find me?"

"Why, I have no idea. I know only that you were in bed. I

lay on your chest. I rode your breathing, up and down. Up and down. I thought to take a cat nap. I closed my eyes. And the next thing I knew, I was no longer there. I was here."

"So somehow you entered my dream."

"I prefer to think that you entered mine, my dear Goose. Or perhaps we are both part of someone else's dream."

"So confusing!"

"Best not to fret. The point is, we are here. We have arrived where we have arrived. And as there's nothing to be gained from loitering in this cave, perhaps we should begin our traveling."

"Yes. Yes. We should go. But—where? And how? I can't see a thing."

He jumped to the ground.

"No fear. We cats have exquisite night vision. I had a moment or two to scout the territory before you dropped in. There's an easy way out, if we just bear left."

"And what's outside?"

"Summer or winter. Night or day. Friend or foe, Goose. It all remains to be seen. I can't begin to guess."

I stood. I stretched. My hands brushed the low ceiling of our cave. I picked up the skipping rope. I knotted it around my waist. I remembered Govan saying once that all he really required in the world was a harp and a rope. "With a harp and a rope there's much a person can do," he said.

I heard his voice in memory, and my heart ached. I imagined Govan and Ebba sitting by my bed, watching me sleep, but knowing nothing of where I was or what I was doing. Oh, I was homesick, then. I sniffed back a tear.

"You must be strong, Goose."

"Yes."

"Shall we go?"

"Yes."

For yes is all you ever need to say to begin a journey. Yes is what I said. And so we started walking.

17

Before we continue

I am 101 years old, and I feel every day of it in my bones. In my long life I have learned many things. I continue to learn. Learning keeps the brain spry. It gives me a reason to get out of bed in the morning. Which is a good thing at any age, but especially at 101. When you're 101, there is sometimes a temptation to just lie still and wait to see what will happen.

Every Saturday afternoon, it has become my habit to make a cup of tea and look back at the week gone by. I review whatever fresh bits of information might have come my way. The name of a bird or a flower. The best way to remove a tomato stain from silk. The Polish word for hedgehog. They are all good, small things to know.

Today is Saturday. The afternoon is rainy and cool. I have fed the stove another log, and it is belching happily. The steam rises from my chamomile tea. The clock has just sounded three. I sit at my kitchen table, my back to the window. Over the past week, I have learned that this writing business is tricky. Trickier than I would ever have imagined.

I had always supposed it must be the easiest thing in the

world to sit down with quill and paper and tell a story. Start at the beginning. Work to the middle. Write to the end. What could be so difficult? But after a week of scribbling, I understand better what authors must endure.

First of all, there are too many words to choose from. There are so many ways to say the same thing. It makes your head hurt trying to settle on just one. And writing is as hard on the hand as it is on the head. It has given me blisters. My wrist has gone stiff. My knuckles are swollen and sore. Finally, no one seems to think of writing as work. People see you hunched over your writing and imagine it is perfectly all right to interrupt you with foolish questions.

Only this morning an annoying young man leaned right through my window. The shadow of his hat—it was made of blue felt and decorated with a huge feather that was suffering ill effects from the rain—fell over my page. These days I am often visited by shadows, but this one was not familiar. I looked up.

"Good morning, grandmother."

Grandmother? What nerve! Better than "Harpy," but only just.

"I am not your grandmother, young man. My name is Penelope, which hardly anyone around here seems to remember."

"So sorry."

"And there's no need to flap your lips in that exaggerated way. You look like a carp that's jumped out of its pond and is drowning in the air. I'm quite capable of lip-reading normal speech. Who are you? What do you want?"

"I'm called Micah. They tell me in the village that you are a harp maker."

"They will tell you lots of things if they think that you will listen. They love nothing better than to gossip with strangers."

"Then it's not true?"

"That I am a harp maker? No. It would be true to say that I *was* a harp maker. But I no longer am. I am 101 years old, young man. I have not made a harp for almost forty years. It is hard work, which is something the tongue-waggers in the village know little enough about."

"Ah. Then perhaps they were also mistaken when they told me that you had many harps in your house?"

"Young man, unless you are as blind as I am deaf, you can see for yourself that that much is so. You can see that that is exactly the case. Look carefully, young man. Those are not bats hanging from the rafters. And those looming figures, the ones against the wall, are not hungry guests waiting to be called for dinner. They are just what they appear to be. That is to say, they are harps. And there are more besides, upstairs and in the cellar. There are some in the shed. I have more than thirty harps."

"More than thirty!"

"As I said. All fine harps, too. All of my own manufacture. I was a harp maker, once upon a time. And I am, and always will be, a harp maker's daughter. My father's name was Govan. You have heard of him, of course."

"I am sorry to say I have not."

"More's the pity when a name like his is forgotten. He was a great man. He worked and lived in this very house. I am the second generation to make harps here. I only made them, mind you. Making them was enough for me. The playing I left to others. Govan did both. There was no one who could coax so beautiful a sound out of wood and string as Govan."

"Your father was your teacher, then?"

"I learned some of what I know from him. The rest I acquired elsewhere."

"Where is elsewhere?"

"That, young man, is a very long story, and not one I'm inclined to tell to strangers, however lovely their hats. Now, if you would excuse me—"

I began to turn back to my writing, but I was not quick enough. I read his words out of the corner of my eye.

"Just one more thing."

He stuck his head farther into the window. Rain dripped from his sodden feather onto my floor.

"Young man, I may be old but I am not idle. I have work to do."

"I'll be quick. I wondered if you had any harps that might be for sale?"

"No. Not a one."

"Oh, come. Out of more than thirty harps there's not one you'd part with? I'd pay you well."

He did have the look of wealth about him. Hats like his do not come cheap.

"As I said, not a one. They are not for sale at any price, and I am not tempted by riches. What need do I have for money at my age? In any case, why do you ask? If you want to play the harp you must begin when you are young. You are already too long in the tooth. And I can't see why you would be interested. The harp has fallen out of fashion. No one plays the harp any more."

He laughed at that.

"It isn't for me, Penelope. The harp is for my daughter. As for fashion, it matters nothing to her. For as long as she has been able to talk, she has asked for a harp."

"You don't say. Where do young people get such ideas? In my day, young man, girls did not play the harp."

"And surely they didn't make them either."

I looked at him closely to see if he was being flip.

"No," I answered sharply. "No, they did not. What is your daughter's name?"

I read a laugh on his lips.

"You will find this an odd coincidence, I feel sure. Her name is also Penelope."

Oh, my! At that news, my old heart skipped a beat, which is perilous when you are 101. I felt my face whiten. A shadow I am coming to know well entered the room and settled in a far corner. I grimaced to see it and trembled with a sudden chill. The Shadow goes nowhere without its friend, the cold.

"Penelope?" asked the man with the feathered cap. "Are you well?"

"Yes, yes. I am fine. Just fine. Where were we? Yes. Yes. You are called Micah and your daughter is called Penelope."

"She is."

"An old-fashioned name for a girl with old-fashioned tastes. How old is she?"

"She will turn eleven next month. I was hoping to surprise her with a harp on her birthday."

What a funny sensation settled over me. I began to think that somehow this was a conversation I'd had before, but many years ago. I felt somehow as if I had one foot in the past and one in the present.

"Eleven next month. You don't say so. Well, well. A big day."

"Yes, indeed. I won't take up more of your time except to ask this. If you can't part with a harp, can you think of someone else who might have such a thing for sale?"

The meddlesome Shadow rose up from its corner and drifted slowly across the room. The chill tightened its grip. I had to concentrate to stop myself from shaking.

"Someone else with a harp for sale. Let me see. No. No, I can't call anyone to mind."

"So there is no hope?"

"Young man, what a foolish thing to say. There is always hope. Always. I shall think on it. Come back next week. Come next Saturday at this same time. I may have something to tell you by then."

And so he went on his way, out into the rain. By now he will have returned home. He will have hung his hat to dry. He will be telling his wife about the strange old lady and her house full of harps. Harpy. Harpy. I closed the window as soon as he had gone. I drew the blinds. I wanted no more interruptions. I wanted to get on with my story. Now my only company is the Shadow. It stays longer every time it visits. It sits quietly by the door.

"Go away."

It won't budge.

"Go away," I repeat, but there it remains. It lingers, for all the world like a cat that asks too often to be let outside.

"You found your own way in. You can find your own way out. But don't think you're welcome here. Don't think I'll pay you any mind. You're on your own. I've too much work to finish to worry about the likes of you."

It settles back on its haunches.

"Have it your own way, then."

I find a shawl. I wrap myself against the cold. I turn my back on my unwanted visitor. I go back to writing.

18

Where We Left Off

Scally and I began our walking. So little light entered the cave that I could scarcely see my hand in front of my face. I stepped gingerly, hoping there would be no rocks to stumble over. Scally trotted ahead with confidence. I trailed after his voice.

"Follow me, Goose. I'll have you out of here in no time. Careful. It becomes very narrow."

It surely did. Before we had gone a hundred paces, I was aware that the cave was pressing in on me. It was as if we were entering the narrow end of a funnel. Soon the walls were not even arms-width apart. The roof sloped, forcing me to bend lower and lower, then lower still. In very short order I was crawling along cold, damp ground. Now and then my hand brushed against something soft and squishy, some small and spongy cave dweller that gurgled a protest and retreated at my touch. I did not allow myself to consider what would happen if we encountered more menacing creatures. A biting scorpion, say. A thick-waisted snake. There would be no escape. There would be no way to run, or even to struggle. The passage was becoming tighter and tighter. I foresaw how soon I would no longer be able to crawl, like a baby. I would have to slither, like a worm.

"Scally!"

He turned his head. I saw the green and golden glow of his eyes.

"Scally, are you sure this way out will be big enough for me?"

"It will have to be, Goose. There is no other way. Follow along."

I had no choice. I followed my four-footed guide, slowly, carefully. I did whatever I could to keep myself from slipping into fearfulness. I tried counting each crawling step but soon lost track. Under my breath I chanted skipping rhymes, but they only excited the futile urge to jump. I tried calling up images of home: my family, my house, my room. How my heart ached! What were they doing now—Ebba, Alloway and Govan? Then I remembered something Govan once said when I felt discouraged. He said, "If you are climbing a mountain, you must always see yourself at the top. If you are running a race, you must always see yourself crossing the line. Believe strongly enough in your vision, and nothing will stop you. What you imagine will become what you achieve."

And so I thought of Sophy. I conjured her face, her voice. I saw the two of us, hand in hand, walking up the path to our house. I saw Ebba running out to greet us, scooping us into her arms, and Govan right behind her, moving as fast as his stiff limbs would allow. I saw Alloway grinning in the doorway, and Cuthbert looking pleased. We are home. We are home. Happy. Happy. I look up to the roof of our house. I see the cat by the chimney pot. He looks back. He winks.

"Stay alert now!"

Scally's voice jerked me back to the here and now. To the dangerous present, which was far, far from home.

"Stay alert, Goose. Here the path begins to rise."

And not just to rise, but to twist and turn. And not just to twist and turn, but to become impossibly narrow and tight. Now I was moving forward by inches. All at once, I was seized by the terrible thought that I would get stuck. I would not be able to advance. I would not be able to go back. Here is where I would end my days. The air left my lungs. I began to gasp. Panic. Panic.

"Scally! Scally! I can't!"

"You must, Goose."

His voice was encouraging but firm.

"You must."

An order.

"Not much farther, now."

Smaller and smaller. Twisting up. Twisting forward. Arms pinned to sides. I imagined an open field. I imagined a wide sky. No good. Then, unbidden, a memory. Another small place, but cozy, warm. Where? Ah! Under the kitchen table. All hidden and secret. How old am I? Four? Five? No older. Sunlight on the fresh-washed floor. The yeasty smell of bread baking. A sucking sound. An infant, nursing. Ebba's friend Gwenlyn has a brand-new baby. "How can so big a bear come from so small a cave?" Gwenlyn says to Ebba. And they laugh a knowing laugh. I look at Ebba's legs. Did I really slither out from between them? Amazing. So big a bear. So small a cave.

"Aha! At last!"

Scally's voice again.

"We're there, Goose. We're there!"

The sudden rush of a cool breeze filled me with vigor. I gave a final kick, like an exhausted swimmer who knows she is almost at the shore. One mighty push and my head popped into clear air. My shoulders followed, then my torso. My legs. My feet. And then I was out. I was in the clear. I lay, exhausted.

"Good work, Goose. Good work."

My eyes were closed. I listened to my heart thudding heavily inside my chest. I felt its racing slow. I opened my eyes. I turned to look at the hole from which we had just emerged. Incredibly, there was nothing there. No opening. No fissure. Nothing at all. There was no way back. There was nowhere to go but on.

"Look around you, Goose," said Scally, "and see where we've fetched up."

I stood. He leapt to my shoulder with a single bound.

"It is beautiful, don't you find?" he asked. He wrapped himself around me like a stole.

From atop a high hill, we looked out on a vast expanse of blue-black sky. It was as if a dark cloak had been opened to reveal a luminous lining. I blinked like a mole that surfaces at noon. Scally was right. It was beautiful. A gibbous moon. Thousands and thousands of stars. They were hung in constellations the likes of which I'd never seen. Stars and moon spilled amber light, illuminating a lovely vista.

Below us lay a valley white with snow. It was criss-crossed with lines, like a great cupped palm. But not even an expert seer would have had time to read the story of our future. Before we could get our bearings, my feet had quit the ground. Suddenly we were airborne and flying fast, carving a path between the rolling snow below and the glittering galaxies above.

19

Into the Valley of Singing Trolavians

One second we had been looking down into the snowy valley. Next thing we knew, we were flying above it. I had never in my life been so surprised. Scally was likewise astonished. He let go an indignant yowl. He found his claws. He sank them deep into my shoulder. He held on for dear life.

We were moving so fast that I hardly noticed his determined grip. My skipping rope, knotted round my waist, trailed behind me like a skinny banner. From this great height, I could see that the valley was surrounded by hills. Beyond the hills was an impressive ring of mountains. Here and there I saw a glimmer of light or smoke from a farmhouse chimney. Once or twice, I made out the antlike figures of citizens going about their business. What was not clear to me was who or what had snagged us.

There were three of them. One was charged with carrying us. The other two flew alongside. They bore no resemblance to anything I had ever seen before. They were spiky and plump, like hedgehogs, with round gray bellies. They had wide wings, all leather and no feather, such as might be found on a gigantic bat. They had long, flexible legs, like those of a hare, and two long, narrow slats, like simple skiis, that served for feet. I straddled the left foot of the creature who ferried us, as though it were a seesaw. I held on as tightly to its shin as Scally held on to my shoulder.

"Goose! Whatever has grabbed us?"

As if in answer, the two escorts began to chant. They traded off lines, batting them back and forth like a ball across a net.

Fall in!
Fall in!
Fall in!
Fall in!
Fall in, three, four,
Tell them what you've told before!
Singing Trolavians, brave and proud
At home in the snow or above the clouds.

"Singing what?" asked Scally.

"Trolavians, I think."

Fall in!
Fall in!
Fall in!
Fall in!
Fall in, five, six,
Tell them what you do for tricks!
Fly in formation with lines so tight
And sing out a fugue while the moon shines bright.

Then they began a complicated round, lobbing snatches of melody at each other across the sky. These Trolavians were very good singers.

Fall in!
Fall in!
Fall in!
Fall in!
Fall in, seven, eight,
Tell them why you can't be late!
Flying is hard but we must be fleet
We are the Guard and we are Elite.

"Goose. Where do you suppose they're taking us?"

I had no answer, although the same question was very much in my mind. I was anxious to find out what the Trolavians intended. Would they welcome us, or throw us in jail? Would they give us a banquet, or put us in a pot and boil us?

"Sergeant Bergus!" sang out the Trolavian to our right, in a strong baritone.

"Captain Fergus!" answered his companion to the left, singing out in a clear tenor voice.

"What do you make of our new recruit? Do you think she is a worthy addition to the Elite Trolavian Guard?"

"I don't know, Captain. She seems rather slow to me. What do you say, Private Belle? Are you rather slow?"

The jibe was aimed at the Trolavian who carried us. All this while she had been silent. Now she sang back her answer in an agitated alto voice.

"I was the fastest flyer in the Transport Division, as you know very well. I earned my promotion and I could keep up with you any day."

"Oh ho! Is that so! Sergeant. Did you hear that?"

"I did, Captain."

"Should we put her to the test, Sergeant?"

"Let's."

And again they began to sing.

Fall out!
Fall out!
Fall out!
Fall out!
Fall out, nine, ten
Make the Private think again!
Slow as a pigeon stuck in a coop,
Let's see her handle a loop the loop.

With that, Fergus and Bergus soared straight up into the air and began to perform a complicated series of acrobatic dives, turns and twists and figure 8's.

"Not fair!" howled Belle.

"What's wrong, Private?" sang the Captain as he swooped past her.

"Can't keep up?" taunted the Sergeant.

"Not fair!" she called again. "You know I'm carrying the prisoners."

"Sad excuse," laughed Bergus, swooping around us as if he were wrapping Belle with ribbon. "If you were truly Elite, you could do this carrying prisoners and wearing a blindfold and with one wing in a sling."

"You're a hopeless case, Belle," sneered Captain Fergus. "How you got into the Elite is a mystery to me. You won't last, Private, mark my words."

"Not fair! Not fair! Not fair!"

"Fair has nothing to do with it. Let's see if you can at least manage a landing. Ready, Sergeant?"

"Ready and steady, sir."

"Hand off the prisoners, Private Belle. And try to do it right. You know how testy the Magistrate becomes when his prisoners are dead on delivery."

"Dead?" gasped Scally. "Oh, Goose, I don't like the sound—"

But before he could finish his sentence, Fergus had sung out another command.

"Private Belle, prepare to jettison cargo."

"Ready to jettison, sir."

"Sergeant Bergus, prepare for cargo retrieval."

"Ready for retrieval, sir."

"On the count of three, Private Belle. One. Two. Three. Tip!"

And as though the two long planks of her feet had been fastened to her ankles with hinges, she angled them so that they pointed straight down towards the snowy valley far, far below. They were no longer parallel to the earth; they were perpendicular to it.

"Goose!" Scally shrieked. My fingers lost their grip on Belle's shin.

"Help!" he cried as we were launched into the eager arms

of gravity. My stomach rose to meet my throat. Scally's howl was so prolonged and shrill that I could scarcely hear Fergus's crisp command.

"Retrieve!"

And in a fraction of a second, Bergus had swooped beneath us. He broke our fall, positioning himself with pinpoint accuracy so that we landed squarely on his flat, broad back.

"Grab fast, Goose," Scally pleaded. I didn't require any urging. I reached out and held firmly onto the sergeant's neck, just as I had once seen some daring boys do on a half-wild horse.

"Transfer completed, sir," reported Bergus, as he joined his companions in their flying formation.

"Excellent work, Sergeant. And an adequate job, Private Belle, although your tipping is far from perfect. I shall have to make a report to the Magistrate."

"But there was nothing wrong with my tipping," Belle sputtered.

"And I will also be mentioning your disregard for constructive criticism, which verges on insubordination."

"But—"

"Enough, Private Belle. Now, prepare to land. On the count of three, execute wing fold. One. Two. Three. Fold!"

In unison, they stopped beating their broad wings and held them close to their sides. In unison, they stopped riding the air and began to plummet towards earth.

"Oh my stars and garters!" yelped Scally as we raced down. I was too petrified to make a sound. But our captors were anything but silent. Fergus and Bergus whooped with delight as they dove. When they touched the snowy slope, the trio of Trolavians erupted into a rippling laugh that bounced, echoing, from hill to hill. We slalomed among those sparkling shards of sound. We skidded along at breakneck speed, still full of the feeling of flying, down and down and down into the valley of the Singing Trolavians.

20

city of snow

In Hamelin, we build our homes from whatever is near to hand. Wood and stone make our walls. Straw gives us thatch for our roofs. Likewise, the Trolavians made use of the raw materials that were most readily available to them. They built from snow. They built from ice.

White buildings on a white landscape washed by the light of moon and stars: the Trolavian city was cunningly camouflaged. I did not even know it was there until we passed through an icy archway. Two Trolavian sentries posted at the gate gave us a stiff salute as we careened past and down a wide boulevard. The street was lined with tall houses, with shops and market stalls.

There was no shortage of other Trolavians out and about. They hummed or whistled or sang as they went about their business. The air was full of the strains of harmony. Upright, the Trolavians were slender of leg and chubby of trunk. Most kept their wings folded about them like cloaks. They propelled themselves by sliding forward on their long, narrow feet, like skating prickly pears.

The Trolavians we passed were smooth and graceful, but

none moved with the purpose and speed of our captors. They whooshed lickety-split down the avenue.

"Get out of the way, you tub of lard, for we're the Elite Trolavian Guard!" Fergus or Bergus would klaxon whenever someone strayed into their path.

"Soldiers!" I heard one mother carol out, in a high soprano, as she scooped her baby up out of harm's way. "Why must they always be so rude?"

"Fergus and Bergus and Belle!" sang out one elderly citizen. "That's dangerous sliding. I'll file a complaint with the Supreme Magistrate."

"I'll give him your regards," laughed Fergus. "Get out of our way, you curs and hounds, the Magistrate's Palace is where we're bound!"

The reckless recruits veered left, then right, while Scally and I clung on for dear life. They scooted into a square where they executed a couple of sweeping loops around a tall obelisk, then dashed up a narrow lane and into a wide plaza.

"Down with the drawbridge, up with the gate, we're the Elite and we can't be late!" they chorused. They sped in the direction of a massive bastion. It stood secure behind a thick, crenellated wall. A flag flew from a high parapet. It was emblazoned with the words "PALACE OF JUST ICE." Two sleepy sentries snapped to attention. They didn't have time to lower the drawbridge, but it hardly mattered. Fergus and Bergus and Belle were moving with such velocity that they quite literally flew across the wide moat. They didn't even flap their wings.

The heavy gates were raised in the nick of time. In a couple of blinks we were inside the fortress. We passed down a long corridor and through an open door. In a cavernous, torch-lit hall, we came to a screeching halt.

"Thank goodness," whispered Scally as we were deposited, with very little ceremony, onto the icy floor.

"Prisoners, attention!" was Bergus's stern command. This was easier said than done. The floor was slippery, and I was dizzy after all that rapid-fire flying and skating. But Bergus didn't give us time to find our land legs.

"Forward, march!"

The hall was empty of furniture, save for an imposing high-backed throne at the far end of the room. The throne had ornately carved arms and legs. It was so large that it almost swallowed the tiny Trolavian who sat upon it. This, evidently, was the Supreme Magistrate. His legs and long feet stuck straight out before him. He held a book that was nearly as large as he. The title on the cover read, "THE LAW, COMPLETE."

The Magistrate squinted down at us. He hummed and whistled in a distracted kind of way. He looked us up and down for a good long moment before he finally addressed us. He may have been small, but his voice was as deep as ever I'd heard.

"Visitors," he sang, in a slow, deliberate way, as if he had had to search hard to find the word to describe us. "Visitors. How uncommon. We are not much in the habit of receiving visitors. Captain Fergus. Explain."

"We discovered them at the border while we were on patrol, Your Supremacy, and made haste to bring them here. They have no passports."

"No passports. Well, well, well. That's very serious. No passports. Tut, tut. Sergeant Bergus, what do you make of them?"

"Strange beings, Your Supremacy, and altogether misshapen. They are both wingless and spikeless. As you can see, one has two legs and one has four, and their feet are badly deformed."

"Yes. Yes. I see that this is so. They have very small feet. Private Belle, what do you think?"

"Well," she began, but Fergus interrupted her.

"They are spies, Your Supremacy!"

"Spies!"

"Spies!"

He and Bergus tossed the word back and forth gleefully. They flapped their wings with excitement.

"No!"

I startled myself by saying it.

"No. We're not spies. How could we be spies? We never meant to come here. We don't even know where we are."

The Guards, surprised into silence by the sound of my voice, stopped their capering. The Magistrate gave us another long look.

"Say again?"

"I said, we're not spies. I am Penelope. This is Scally. And we don't even know where we are, except that we are in a dream. Your Supremacy," I added, as an afterthought. My voice trailed away. In a dream? Why had I said so? They would think me mad.

I expected the Magistrate to look scornful. But his face had softened. He had lost his sneer of cold command. Slowly, slowly, he smiled.

"Ah," he sang, deep and clear. "Of course. I ought to have

known. You have come on behalf of Cuthbert, haven't you? Yes. I understand. At last, you have come."

21

A Magician Had Two Sons

Something had changed. We were no longer prisoners now, but welcome guests. We were ushered into the Magistrate's private chambers. He invited us to sit at a banquet table bedecked with candles and laden with food. The Magistrate sat at the head of the table. Fergus and Bergus and Belle stood watchfully behind him. For the first time since we had arrived in his snowy precinct, I was aware of the cold. The shock of so much newness had dulled my mind to the fact that I was wearing only a plain shift and simple sandals. Now I shivered and hugged myself. I rubbed my arms to keep warm.

"You are chilled. Cloak yourself in this," said the Magistrate. He handed me a taupe-colored wrap that was mottled with green. I wrapped it around me like a shawl, and was pleased to find that, though it was light as air, it provided wonderful protection against the cold. Scally cuddled under it too, close to my chest.

"How lovely," he purred. "I wouldn't have expected to find silk in this place."

"We have no silk here," answered the Magistrate. "That is dragon leather."

I must have looked incredulous, because he laughed, rich and deep.

"Yes, Penelope. Dragon leather. Dragons live just beyond our borders, on the other side of the mountains."

"Are they dangerous?" I asked, fingering the soft shawl. I had always imagined dragons to be scaly and rough.

"Dangerous? By and large, no. They suffer from not knowing their own strength, which can sometimes be hazardous, as much for them as for others."

"Then why do you kill them?"

Fergus and Bergus giggled when they heard this, but the Magistrate silenced them with a glance.

"We don't."

"But surely to get the skin to make the leather . . ."

"No, no," answered the Magistrate. "Trolavians are neither hunters nor war-makers. We are a peaceful folk. But dragons are rather dim. They get lost very easily. They might be picking mushrooms or gathering wildflowers, and they will completely lose track of their whereabouts. They panic. They run. Dragons are tireless and fleet. They dash about in ever-widening circles. Sometimes they gallop so far and so fast that they will cross over the mountains and into our valley. Usually, they are discovered by a border patrol and turned back. An unfortunate few, however, pass undetected. Theirs is a warm and balmy country. They cannot last long in our climate."

"They die?"

"Sadly, yes."

"Poor things," I said. I felt deeply sorry for whatever dragon had frozen to death so far from home and been reduced to the hide I now wore about my shoulders.

"Poor things, true enough. But once it has happened, there

is nothing to be done. We Trolavians are as practical and thrifty as we are musical. Rather than let the dragons go to waste, we tan the hide. We eat the flesh."

"Oh, dear," said Scally quietly, for we were at that moment enjoying a reviving feast of carrots and parsnips and some obscure meat on skewers.

While we ate, I told the Magistrate about Hamelin, about the rats, about the Piper. I told him about the missing children, about my deafness. I told him about my gift of Deep Dreaming. It all seemed so extraordinary that I could hardly believe my own words as I spoke them. But he listened carefully, nodding, now and then asking a question. When finally my tale was done and our plates were cleared away, I felt bold enough to ask a question of my own.

"Your Supremacy, how is it that you know our friend Cuthbert?"

He smiled.

"We have known Cuthbert for many, many years. I will answer your question, Penelope, but first you must hear a story. It is a strange tale to tell, although it is well known hereabouts. Fergus and Bergus and Belle would have heard it from the time they were babies. It is, in some ways, the story of how we Trolavians came to be."

A small, happy sigh issued from the Guards. Whatever the story he referred to, it was apparently a tale they hadn't tired of hearing.

"Once upon a time," began the Magistrate, "in a land that was neither yours nor mine, there lived a powerful magician. He had two sons. His wife died giving birth to the second one.

The magician never remarried. He raised the boys himself. It was his wish that they learn his craft. The old man used his power for good, and he desired that his sons do the same. He taught them spells to bring good fortune. He instructed them in charms to comfort the heartbroken. He showed them herbs and plants that could help heal the sick.

"One day, the magician himself fell ill. None of his incantations or remedies could prevent his own failing. It was whispered that some practitioner of the dark arts, a wizard even stronger than he, had laid a curse on him. Perhaps that was so. Perhaps it was not. All that is certain is that he sickened. And then died.

"The magician passed away before his sons were fully grown. Had he lived longer, he might have been able to nurture the seeds of goodness he had planted within them. Indeed, in the younger boy the seeds sprouted. They took root and grew. But in the older, they withered away.

"After his father's death, the younger son set off on a long journey. There was no reason for him to stay. According to the custom of that place, the magician's house and all his possessions went to the firstborn. The elder son could easily have shared his inheritance, but he showed no inclination to do so. The younger son accepted this with good grace. He welcomed the chance for adventure. He embraced his brother. He embraced his fate. He wandered.

"Now, the good old magician had many books. Some contained the secrets of black magic. The oldest son, with no one to prevent it, began to study them. The more he read, the hungrier he became for the power they promised. One day, in a dusty old volume, he came upon a spell that amused him. This incantation promised to change a simple reed into an instrument that would give the player control over all who heard it. When first he read the charm, the eldest son laughed. He thought it a frivolous fancy. Nonetheless, he chose a reed. He made his flute. He uttered the prescribed words. He put the reed to his lips. He played."

The Magistrate paused.

"I think by now you will know of whom I speak."

"It can only be the Piper."

And when I said "the Piper" there was a sharp sucking in of air by the Guards behind the Magistrate's chair. They fluttered their wings and repeated his name, a whispered, fearful echo.

The Piper, the Piper, the Piper.

"Indeed," said the Magistrate. "The Piper. And by now you know how successful the spell was. At first he treated his flute as a toy. He would use it to charm birds so that they would pluck him the choicest fruit from the highest branches. He would cause mice to somersault across the table, or make bears bring him his firewood. He had not yet tested its greater powers.

"Then, one day, the younger brother returned for a visit. He had practiced diligently everything his father had taught him. He had grown stronger in his goodness. The older boy was not glad to see his brother. He knew his sibling would disapprove of the path he had chosen to follow. Even so, he could not stop himself from bragging about his new powers. He could not stop himself from showing off. He used his pipe to make a squirrel dust a bookshelf with its long tail. He made a fox dance in the moonlight. It was a silly game, but it troubled the younger brother. He saw clearly enough where all this would lead. He knew his brother would not be swayed. He knew he must think of a way to stop him. And so he made a plan. He waited until the moment was right.

"One night, the two young men lay in their beds. They talked back and forth, just as they had done when they were little boys. They shared memories of childhood and of their father. Memories of the stories he had told them. Of the games they had played.

" 'What were they called,' the younger brother asked, 'those creatures he invented when he told us bedtime stories? Do you remember?'

" 'Trolavians,' laughed his older brother. 'They had faces and bellies like trolls, and legs and wings like birds.'

" 'Yes! And they lived under a perpetual moon.'

" 'And everything in their country was made of snow and ice.'

" 'And they sang rather than spoke. They were the Singing Trolavians.'

" 'Silly stories!' laughed the older brother.

" 'Perhaps. But Father had his reasons for telling them. Do you remember how he used those stories to get us to practice Deep Dreaming?'

" 'Of course. He would tell us a Trolavian bedtime story. Then we would sleep and slip into Trolavian dreams.'

" 'We had contests. Who could get there first. Who could stay the longest.'

" 'Yes,' said the older brother, 'and I recall that it was always I who won.'

" 'You had the advantage. Your gift for Deep Dreaming was greater than mine.'

" 'Yes, brother. It was. It still is!'

" 'Do you think so? Such things can change, you know.'

" 'Is that a challenge, little one?'

" 'Oh, no. Not a challenge. Think of it as a contest for old time's sake. If your powers are as great as you claim, you have nothing to fear from the likes of me.'

" 'Very well. Let us sleep, and reconvene among the Trolavians.'

"They slept," continued the Magistrate. "They dreamed. They came, each in his turn, to the land of the Trolavians."

A clock chimed then, somewhere in the distance. Twelve slow gongs drifted across the cold Trolavian air. Scally opened his mouth and yawned, clean and wide. He tried to hide it, but the Magistrate saw.

"Excuse me," said Scally, embarrassed.

I had quickly grown accustomed to the melodic rise and fall of Trolavian speech, and it was jarring to hear words spoken, rather than sung. The Magistrate chuckled at Scally's apology, and even his laugh was made of music.

"You might well yawn, Scally. It is late. You have both come far, and you have farther still to go. You must rest. Belle will show you to your room. In the morning, she will accompany you on your way."

There was a joint gasp from Fergus and Bergus. Belle gaped in astonishment. Fergus stepped forward.

"Begging your pardon, sir, but Belle is a very junior member of the Elite Guard."

"I am aware of that, Captain Fergus."

"Meaning only to say, sir," continued Bergus, "that she has only very recently been promoted to our ranks and has very little experience. In the field, I mean."

"Thank you, Sergeant Bergus. I am aware of this as well."

"Which is to say, sir, that she has never flown a solo mission before, and might not be prepared to handle a dangerous—"

"Fergus and Bergus. My mind is made up. Belle will accompany our friends tomorrow. She will take them to the border. She will send them on their way. It is an important assignment, but not a difficult one. And if she does her job well, she will be promoted to the rank of Corporal. I have every confidence in her. That will be all. You two are dismissed."

"Yes, Your Supremacy," they grumbled in unison. They bowed, turned, and made their way out of the room.

"My apologies," said the Magistrate when they had gone. "They are good soldiers but rather hot-headed. I am leaving you in very good hands. Am I not, Private Belle?"

Belle was so flabbergasted that she could only nod her answer.

"To bed, then. Good night."

"Your Supremacy! The story! What happened?" I asked. "What happened to the Piper? What happened to his brother? And how does Cuthbert figure in all of this?"

The Magistrate smiled. "Patience is always rewarded, my friends. You will have your answers soon enough. Belle, would you show our guests upstairs?"

He rose. He made his way from the hall, skating serenely over the icy floor.

"Right," sang Belle, in her rich alto. "Come along, then."

She squared her shoulders in a take-charge way and led us, climbing on her long, slender feet, up a spiraling stairway to our high attic room.

22

The Moon in the Mirror

In my house are many harps, but only one mirror. It sits on my dressing table. It is old, older even than I. Its glass has grown cloudy over the years. It takes in my reflection but returns only a misty shadow. I am just as glad. If you live to be 101, you will probably find that you have seen quite enough of your own face. I am no longer eager to study my complexion. For what will I see if I look closely? Only that I have grown more wrinkles. They crosshatch my face in all directions. They connect up with my scar, like small tributaries that feed a wide river.

Harpy, Harpy, Scarface, wrinkled like a prune,
Harpy, Harpy, Scarface, older than the moon.

That is the summation of evil-minded Mellon and his feckless, stupid crew. They are not far from wrong, of course. Even so, their words are hurtful. If they knew where I'd been and what I've seen, they wouldn't be so quick with their insults. I can always take comfort, when comfort I require, in knowing that their lives will never be half of what mine has been. They will never be called upon to rescue their friends and neighbors. It is unlikely they will ever test their courage, ever know real danger. Certainly, they will never travel through dreams with a talking cat. And they will never have the pleasure of hearing the Trolavians sing. Whenever Mellon and his pea-brained gang pass across my vision, whenever I see those vicious words scrawled across their lips, I think of Belle and the moon song she sang all those years ago.

I am 101 years old. Even so, I remember as if it were yesterday how Belle led Scally and me to our room at the top of the Palace of Just Ice. The moon shone in through a high window. A fire burned in the grate. I was glad to see that there was a thick fur robe on the bed. I wasted no time crawling under it. Scally arranged himself around my shoulders.

"Sleep well," said Belle. "I will wake you in the morning."

"I shall look forward to that," Scally said. "A city made of snow and ice must truly sparkle when the sun shines."

"Sun? Oh, no. We have no sun here. We leave sunshine to the dragons. Trolavians prefer the moon and the stars."

"The sun never shines?"

"Never."

"But how do you tell when night ends and day begins?"

"It is easy. Day begins when breakfast is ready. I shall bring you yours early, so now you must sleep. I will send you on your way with a lullaby. This is the Trolavian Hymn to the Moon."

Perfect, round and golden,
Sister of the stars
Beaming down upon us,
Shining from afar.

Shine down all your blessings,
Shine on house and farm.
Keep us safe from evil,
Keep us safe from harm.

"Beautiful," sighed Scally, who had closed his eyes and struck up a thrumming purr.

"Sweet dreams, Penelope," said Belle. She bent over, as if to kiss me goodnight, but then stopped herself. Perhaps she thought it would be too unsoldierly. Instead, she brushed my head lightly with her strong wing. I smiled as I watched her tiptoe from the room on her skinny feet.

I lay with my eyes open. The room was bright with moonlight, but that was not what kept me awake. My thoughts were like a complicated knot, bristling with loose ends. What had happened to the Piper and his brother? How had Scally and I come to this place? And where would we go from here?

"Sweet dreams," Belle had said. But how was sleep possible when there was so much to untangle? In any case, wasn't I *already* asleep? Wasn't I already in the middle of a dream? What's more, it was not even a dream of my own making. I had not thought up the Trolavians. They were a story told by an old magician to amuse his sons. They had taken the story and turned it into a dream. Somehow, thanks to my strange gift, I had crossed the border into a country that they had invented.

If I were to close my eyes and sleep, here in the land of Trolavians, would I not become a dreamer within a dream within a dream? Where and how would it end? It could go on and on forever and forever. What would happen to me then?

Would I dwindle and grow dim? Would I simply disappear?

"Like mirrors within mirrors," I said to myself. And as if I had spoken a spell, the radiant Trolavian moon sent a sudden, cool beam into the tall looking-glass in the corner of the room. Redoubled, the ghostly light was so bright I had to shield my eyes. The mirror seemed to vibrate and shiver, like a still pond that has just received the gift of a pebble.

Fearful but curious, I disentangled myself from Scally, who was snoring quite loudly by now. I approached the mirror cautiously, tiptoeing across the icy floor. When I finally stood before it, I saw myself reflected there. But not the Penelope I expected to see. No, it was the sleeping Penelope who was contained within the mirror, lying on her bed in Hamelin. Ebba knelt beside her, holding her hand. Govan sat on the other side of the bed, his hand on her brow. Her fat cat, Scallywaggle, was asleep on her chest. Perched on his stool at the foot of her bed was Alloway, who fingered a tune on his harp. The old dog Ulysses lay at his feet.

The image was hazy, as if seen through the waves of heat that rise from red embers. Full of longing for everything I had left behind, I reached out as if to embrace them all. The image shifted, as though the movement of my hands had muddied the waters. Now, a kind old face smiled out at me from the distant world of the waking. It was the face of a friend, of someone I now knew would always be true to his word.

23

who comes through glass

Look for me in glass.

That is what he had told me. And now here he was.

"Cuthbert!"

"You have done well, Penelope. My confidence in you was not misplaced."

"Oh, I am so happy to see you. And to hear you, too. I have my ears back, Cuthbert. And Scally is with me. He talks! In this place, he talks!"

"I hope the Trolavians have treated you kindly. They are not much accustomed to receiving visitors."

"Then you know of the Trolavians? Have you been here, Cuthbert?"

"Once or twice. Do they sing as tunefully as ever?"

"Every word."

"And do they still tell the story of the magician and his two sons?"

"Yes."

"Then you know something of the beginnings of the Piper."

"Yes. The Magistrate told us that he fell in love with black magic and cast the spell to make his flute. He wanted more power, and his brother wanted to stop him before he grew too strong. They came here in a dream, and something happened. But what?"

"Listen carefully, Penelope. I am old and weak and I cannot linger long in this mirror. Everything happened just as the Magistrate told it. The two brothers decided to visit the Trolavians, as they had done when they were boys. But what the Piper could not know was that his brother had paid the Trolavians a solitary visit the night before. He had told the Magistrate everything. He had asked for assistance. The Magistrate assured him the Trolavians would help however they could.

"When the Piper and his brother closed their eyes that night, the Piper fell immediately into a deep trance. He dreamed. He traveled. But the younger brother only pretended to sleep. Behind shut lids, he stayed wide awake. He waited until he knew his brother had reached the Trolavian border.

"Arriving quickly, the Piper made to saunter across the border, as he had done so easily many times before. But the Guards, acting on the Magistrate's orders, announced that there were new rules and regulations for entry. He would have to answer their questions. What is your business here? How long do you intend to stay? Do you understand that it is strictly prohibited to import oranges? They detained the Piper for more than an hour, and that was all the time the younger brother needed to put his plan into action.

"The boys' mother had owned a harp, which she loved and played beautifully. When she died, her husband covered her harp and stored it in a locked room. He could not bear to look on it, for it broke his heart to be reminded of her. That night, the younger brother fetched the harp and brought it to the room where the Piper lay sleeping. He set it beside his brother's bed, then spoke some words he had learned from the old magician's books. Slowly, carefully, and with sadness in his heart, he uttered a spell that set the harp to playing. No fingers plucked its strings, yet it sang out a sweet and ringing melody.

"The music was enchanting. It rippled like a brook in the meadow. It hummed like the south wind in high trees. And its magic was to weave a spell of sleeping so that the object of the enchantment would not wake for as long as the music played. This was the root of the young man's plan. By placing the harp next to the Piper's bed, and by speaking the spell, he cast his own brother into a prison whose walls were made of sleep. The Piper would be locked away, confined to the world of his dreams. The younger brother was deeply aggrieved to take such drastic measures. But he knew his brother was headed in the direction of great harm, and he could think of no other way to stop him.

"He kissed his brother's brow for the last time, then rushed down the stairs and out into the evening air. As he faced the house, he spoke one last spell. He blinked away the tears as a dense and sudden tangle of vines, with stalks thicker than jail bars, grew up around his boyhood home. Then he turned and ran, and wherever his hurrying feet touched the ground, a stand of tall trees reared up behind him. He ran for miles and miles, until finally he fell to the earth, exhausted."

I listened to Cuthbert's story with all my being. So much to absorb! He spoke with great urgency, his words like steam escaping from a boiling kettle.

"But Cuthbert," I asked when he paused for a breath, "what has happened? How is it that the Piper is in the world again?"

"How? Because of a sad truth, Penelope. A spell is only as good as the magician who casts it. The magician who imprisoned the Piper was far from perfect. He was unpracticed. He was young. His heart was full of grief. There was much he failed to take into account."

"Such as?"

"That his powers would weaken with the passing of the years. That the spell he cast upon the harp would start to fray, and the harp's music begin to dwindle. As the magician grows weaker, the music grows slower and softer, and sleep loosens its grip on the Piper. It becomes easier for him to part the curtain that separates the waking from the dreaming world, easier and easier to pass between them. Before long, the harp will fall silent. The Piper will wake. The Piper, who has been so carefully hidden from view that not even Time has found him. Unlike his brother, he has not aged. He is still young. He is still strong. And he is angry. That you can count on."

"What will happen when he wakes?"

"We must never find out."

Cuthbert's image began to blur and fade.

"I must go now, Penelope."

"Wait!"

"Godspeed."

And then where Cuthbert's face had been I saw only my own reflection, wide-eyed and pale. My knees knocked and my teeth chattered as I climbed back into bed and under the fur robe. Scally stretched and stirred, but he did not wake. I held him to my chest as I stared up at the perpetual moon. I lay awake until what passed for morning dawned in the land of the Singing Trolavians.

24

A Truth Revealed

"This is where I will leave you," sang Belle.

We stood in moonlight on a narrow mountain plateau. Above us loomed a snowy peak. We were so high up that whatever land lay beneath was obscured by clouds. They stretched on and on before us, in furrows, like a field. In the distance they glowed pink, a sign that somewhere, high in the sky of the country for which we were bound, there was sun.

"Thank you for all your kindness," said Scally. He stretched. He yawned. He licked his paw. He fussed with his whiskers. "It was a very smooth ride."

"The pleasure was mine," Belle answered with a blush and a funny, formal bow. "I'm glad you were comfortable. I wish I could accompany you farther. But I have never been outside my own realm. There are dragons. There is sunshine. I would not feel welcome. I can do nothing more than wish you well, and offer you some nourishment before you continue. I have brought some small provisions."

Food was a welcome proposition. We had been flying for hours over the snowy countryside, nestled in a basket Belle had attached to herself by way of a harness. I was very glad of the dragon-skin wrap, which the Magistrate had insisted I take along on the journey. We had met again in his private chambers before setting out.

"You will find it useful, I am certain," he had said. "You are not yet accustomed to this chilly place, and you risk catching cold on the long flight ahead. Perhaps you will have a chance to get some rest. You don't look to me like someone who has enjoyed a good sleep."

His face was so kind, and the wink he sent me so knowing, that I blurted out everything I had seen and heard. He listened closely. He nodded. He seemed anything but surprised.

"Poor Cuthbert," he said. "It saddens me to think that he has grown so old."

"Please tell me how you know him."

"Cuthbert is a friend of long standing, although we have not seen one another for many years."

"And it was true, everything he told me?"

"Cuthbert was never one to lie. It happened as he said. We detained the Piper here while the spell was cast. When he found that he was unable to return to the world of the waking, he ranted and roared. He shrieked out all kinds of terrible threats. We were not afraid. We Trolavians are made of music, and his pipe has no power over us. We insisted that he leave our country, and when last we saw him, he was stalking through the snow, calling out insults and curses."

"What became of him? Where is he now?"

"That I cannot tell you. I only know that he established his own small realm, somewhere well beyond our borders. And now you must continue your journey. Belle will take you as far as she is able."

"May I trouble you with one last question?" I asked the Magistrate, as we settled into the basket.

"By all means."

"It's Cuthbert. How does he fit into the puzzle?"

The Magistrate considered my question in silence a long time.

"I have been reluctant to tell you the whole of it. But of course, you have a right to know. It was Cuthbert who wound the spring that set all this in motion."

"I don't understand."

"Who spoke the words. Who cast the spell. Who then grew old."

"You mean to say that—"

"Yes, Penelope. And now you must save your sister. You will find her in the keeping of Cuthbert's brother."

For the whole time of our flying, and even after we had landed on the high plateau, I turned these words over and over in my mind and heart. The Piper's brother. What a burden to have borne all those years.

"Penelope!"

Belle's clear voice broke into my thoughts.

"You must have something to eat before continuing on your way."

She had spread a blanket on the ground and laid a picnic upon it, humming and whistling as she set things just so.

"Just light fare," she explained, apologetically.

"You must be very hungry after all that flying," said Scally.

"Not at all. That was nothing. When I was with the Transport Corps, I went much farther with much heavier loads. I was the best soldier they had, fast and strong. That's how I won my promotion to the Elite Trolavian Guard. Of course, I'm only a Private, but I aspire to much, much more."

Her eyes were dreamy, and I supposed she was imagining the day she made General.

"At least you'll be promoted to Corporal soon," said Scally. "That's a start."

"Yes," she sang happily. "Now, have some food. Lemonade and shortbread. You cannot leave us without sampling our shortbread. It is a Trolavian specialty."

"Why are they green?" asked Scally, when she opened the tin.

"Silly question," she chortled. Her laugh was a rippling trill. "All shortbread is green. If it's not green, it's not shortbread."

We each took a biscuit.

"My," said Scally, very pleased. "Shortbread is not my usual line of thing, but this is delicious."

"Very tasty," I agreed. Belle beamed. I was sorry she would not be coming with us. I was certain that she would be a source of great good cheer. What's more, I was not at all looking forward to our descent from this high mountain. It would surely be a long walk, and probably a dangerous one.

"They *are* tasty," said Belle. "If ever I start to doubt that there is still such a thing as goodness in the world, I think about shortbread. Shortbread and singing. That is all the evidence I need to prove that someone, something, somewhere, watches over us."

"Singing is a gift," I said. "My sister has a beautiful voice."

Sophy! Where was she now? My face must have betrayed my thoughts, for Belle clucked sympathetically.

"You will find her, I am sure. You will see her home again.

I'm sorry I shan't be able to meet her. I would like to hear her sing."

"Like an angel," said Scally. "She sings like an angel."

"And you, Penelope? Do you also sing?"

"No, Belle." I laughed. "I love music, but I have a voice like a rusty hinge."

"How sad! I can't imagine not singing. Mind you, no Trolavian would want to go on living if she couldn't sing. I imagine you could at least yodel, Penelope."

"Yodel? Oh, no. I don't think so."

"Why not? Anyone can learn to yodel. I could teach you if you'd like."

Belle rose from the blanket. She stood on her long legs. She tilted back her head, as if she were preparing to gargle. She opened her mouth and released the most extraordinary sound.

"Yodel-odel-odel-oda-leydee-ooooooooo! Yodel-odel-odel-oda-leydee-ooooooooo!"

It bounced from mountain peak to mountain peak and back again.

"Now you."

"Oh, Belle. I can't."

"Of course you can. Scally, you too."

Plainly she would give us no peace until we joined her ululations. And so, laughing, we threw back our heads. We opened our throats.

"Yipa-yipa-yopa-oola-yee-a-hooooooooo! Yipa-yipa-yopa-oola-yee-a-hooooooooo!"

"Excellent work," praised Belle, and we would surely have gone on were it not for an ominous rumble.

"What's that?"

The rumbling grew louder. It became a shaking of the earth. We looked towards the summit only to see that much of the snow there had been dislodged by our happy bellowing. Belle had just enough time to cry out, "Avalanche!" before we were swept up by wave upon wave of powdery white and ushered, with great speed and no ceremony, down the mountain.

25

A second visit

Govan always told his apprentices that a harp was like a true friend. "It is not demanding," he would say, "but it cannot be ignored. It has few requirements, but you must pay attention to its needs. Otherwise, it will one day betray you. Do not leave your harp by the heat of the hearth. Keep it away from windows and out of the damp. And most important of all, you must keep it always in tune. A harp left too long out of tune forgets how to sing. Its voice grows hoarse. It will rattle and moan, rather than revel in the harmonious union of wood and string. Anyone who owns a harp, whether or not he plays, sins against it if he does not keep it in tune." And so it is that, with my father's voice in my head, at the age of 101, I keep in tune my many harps.

Cherry and beech and oak. Balsam and larch and ash. Woods that are hard, woods that are soft, woods with grains both fine and coarse. Some are better suited to the business of becoming a harp than others, but none is impossible, and in every piece of wood that comes your way there lives a different spirit. Some are humorous. Some are dark. Some are kindly. Some are full of mischief. Knowing how to read the spirit of the wood is the most important gift a harp maker can possess. It is only when you know the deep, deep secrets of wood that you know how to shape and carve, to bend and plane, so that the harp the wood is destined to become will tell the truth when finally you are done.

Telling the truth is what this writing business is all about, too, or so it seems to me. What is the point of setting down all these words if, in the end, they don't tally up to the truth? Perhaps it is all this truth-telling that has put me in the mood for freeing myself of some of my secrets. I have kept them for many, many years, and they grow heavy. And so I will tell you—I have never spoken of this before—that all my harps have names. Rosamund. Titus. Jasperina. Corinth. It wasn't I who decided on these. Ondine. Clarice. Bertrand the Bold. Johannes the Mild. The harps chose their own names. They revealed them to me when they were ready.

This morning, as I was tuning Madame de la Corde, the beam of sunlight passing through my window was broken by a shadow. Feather, hat and head. I knew very well who it was before I looked up to see the salutation on his lips.

"Ho, Penelope!"

Micah. Had a week already passed since his last visit?

"Ho, yourself."

"That is a very handsome harp."

"Thank you. She is an old lady, and speaking as one myself, I can tell you that such compliments are both rare and welcome."

"And how can you be certain that this harp is not an old gentleman?"

"One knows. When one makes them, one knows. It is as simple as that. Don't dally at the window. I'd rather you came in than have you block my light."

In truth, I was not unhappy to see him. That he kept his promise to return in seven days' time spoke well of him. And I admit that I was flattered, a little, by his respectful attention. He had a pleasing demeanor, and if one *must* entertain guests, they might as well be easy to look at. He sat at my table and we passed a pleasant hour, speaking of this and that.

"Tell me, Penelope. How is it that you can tune your harps when you can't hear?"

"Why, you tell me, Micah. How many doors does your house have?"

"One in front and one in back."

"And do you use one more than the other?"

"The front."

"Which is the usual way. But just as there is more than one way to enter a house, so there is more than one way to welcome sound. It needn't come in through the front door, which for most people would be the ears."

"Where, then, if not through the ears?"

"Every sound vibrates, and no sound vibrates like any other. I can sense those vibrations with my fingers, as though they were a kind of warmth. I know one from another. I know exactly how each should feel. If a note from a harp is even a tiny fraction low or high, my fingers tell the tale."

"And this you learned from your father?"

"No. This I learned from my other great teacher."

"And that is?"

"Time."

"I see," he said. "And tell me, how much more time will pass before you make up your mind?"

"About the harp for your Penelope?"

"Yes."

"I would like to meet the child. Bring her here next week, and we shall see what we shall see."

"Very well. In a week then. May I be permitted one last question?" he asked, which made me laugh.

"I hardly think I could stop you, Micah."

"Your shawl. From what material is it made? I've never seen anything quite like it."

"No. No, you wouldn't have. It is unique."

That is all I revealed to him of the story of the shawl. But you shall hear the rest.

26

Avalanche

Before my untoward elevening—when the Piper came and when my gift of Deep Dreaming was revealed—I had thought my only talent was for skipping. I have already said that I was untouchable. You would never guess it to look at me now, but in my day no one was better at jumping rope than Penelope. My bones may be brittle, but my toes still twitch with remembered eagerness when I think of those rhymes.

Pick a rosy apple
Pick a yellow lemon
Pick the perfect partner
And skip right into heaven!
Pick a tasty mango
Pick a juicy orange
Find a rhyme for that
And you can have my morning porridge!
Porridge doesn't rhyme with orange
Try and you will fumble
You can have my porridge
If you skip and never stumble.

If a skipping ditty had been a promise, I would have had more porridge than I ever could have eaten. I could skip and skip and skip and skip and never, ever stumble. But in the world of Deep Dreaming, I more than stumbled. I lost any chance of holding ground. Our yodeling had released an avalanche, and for the second time since my travels began, I was tumbling. I was tumbling down fast.

The snow was an unstoppable force. Scally jumped onto my shoulder. Belle cried, "Hang on!" I grabbed for her long legs. She flapped her wings and tried to lift us up, but it was too late. We were caught up in the great current, like tiny currants in an enormous mixing bowl. I heard Scally yowl, then felt him wrenched from my shoulder. The snow stopped up my mouth when I tried to call out. Belle struggled valiantly, but there was nothing she could do against the force of the slide.

People will talk of how, in times of great danger, their lives passed before their eyes. I had often heard that expression, but thought it was just a fancy. I wouldn't have believed that such a thing could happen. But I can assure you that it does. Buffeted by snow and plummeting down, I saw my whole life, all my eleven years, as though they were a play, acted out in fast motion. I saw my friends and family. I saw happy times and sad times. I saw the trivial and the consequential. I saw events I thought I had long since forgotten. They flooded my vision, helter skelter, until finally the pictures froze and I could see only my own self, lying in my bed at home.

Bed. Home. How I longed to return. And I felt a surge of anger at that sleeping girl, that Penelope who was both me and not me. I wanted to shake her. I wanted to say, "This is your dream! Do something! Save us!" And then, as though she had heard my wish, I was pulled from the rampaging snow. I was yanked from its tide like a fish. My shift snagged on something, and I was caught fast. I struggled for air as the big breakers of snow rolled over me. I was like an island, firmly anchored, fixed on the map in the middle of an angry ocean.

I had no sense of passing time. I had seen my whole life. Now, my memories were exhausted. Come to that, so was I. I felt so, so tired. There was nothing around me but white, white, white. I wrapped it around me, like a blanket. I closed my eyes. For the first time since I began my dreaming, I slept.

Section iv

A Skipping Dragon

27

whackity

A sound woke me. Something both known and unknown. A distant, rhythmic clatter.

Whack, whack, whackity whack!

I opened my eyes.

Whackity whack! Whackity whack! Whack, whack, whack!

I blinked. I looked around. I took stock. Everything had changed. I had traded a world of tumbling white for a world of dappled green. Green above. Green below. Lovely leaves. I had come to rest in a tall, broad tree. I sat astride a wide branch. The foliage was dense, but here and there a narrow yellow beam shone through. I reached out. It was warm. Sunlight! Whatever place this was, it was far removed from the land of the Trolavians. And whatever place this was, I seemed to be quite alone. I saw no sign of Scally or Belle. Nor could I see the source of the sound.

Whacka! Whacka! Whacka!

I felt remarkably well, all things considered. My limbs were still in place. So was Alloway's necklace. And the skipping rope was still knotted around my waist.

Whackity! Whackity! Whackity!

I knew that sound. Where had I heard it before? It was loud and getting louder. Whoever or whatever was responsible for making it was drawing nearer. The branch seemed very sturdy. It was wide enough to crawl along and didn't bend under my weight. I crept forward, parting leaves, until finally

I was able to look down. So high! Far below was a forest floor. Some small drifts of snow and a few broken branches were the only evidence that the avalanche had passed this way.

Whack, whack, whackity whack!

A pretty footpath had been carved through the forest. It wound among the trees. From my vantage point, it looked like a fallen ribbon. Coming along this path, passing in and out of view, was the source of the rhythmic whacking. Again I blinked. I stared. At first, I couldn't believe my eyes. I had never seen such a creature before, but I knew right away what to name it, for its hide looked exactly like the cloak given me by the Magistrate. There was no doubt. This was a dragon. It was not much taller than I, and it was moving along at a brisk pace. To see a dragon was astonishing enough. More amazing still was that it was not merely walking, not merely promenading trippingly along like a happy Sunday stroller. It was skipping.

Whackity whack! Whackity whack! Whackity whackity whackity whack!

No wonder that sound had seemed so familiar. The dragon was jumping rope as it came along the path. It paused in its travels directly beneath my tree. It sang.

Once there was a dragon and her name was Mary Jane.
She skipped into the forest and was never seen again.
She skipped into the forest and she simply disappeared.
You'll never, ever find her if you search a hundred years.
Skip and never find her, skip and never see!
Mary Jane has vanished now and happy she will be.

Then, with a call of "one, two, three, jolly-o pepper!" the dragon began to skip very quickly. It doubled, then redoubled its speed. It did some fancy foot- and handwork and then proceeded once again—*whackity whack, whackity whack*—along the forest path.

Skip and never find her, skip and never see!
Mary Jane has vanished now and happy she will be.

Was this Mary Jane? I supposed so, although it seemed an unsatisfactory name for a dragon. Had anyone asked me what I thought a dragon might be called, I would have suggested Hermione or Rondella or Peregrine or Sybil. Whatever her name, she was an expert skipper. She would be a worthy opponent in a jumping contest.

The avalanche had thoughtfully deposited me in a tree with branches as evenly spaced as rungs on a ladder. I was down it in a flash and hurrying along the path in pursuit of the skipping dragon. It seemed the only thing to do. I had to find Scally and Belle. And Mary Jane might have seen some trace of them.

The shady woods were silent. Now and then, I heard the raucous shout of what sounded like a crow, but otherwise there was no bird song. Here and there, the thick canopy of leaves parted to allow some sunlight to reach the forest floor. It shone golden and round, as welcome and surprising as a found coin. I jogged along as quickly as I could behind Mary Jane, but the distance between us grew wider. The *whackity whack* of her skipping, which at first had made her easy to follow, was growing fainter and fainter. I supposed that she was picking up speed. The Magistrate had said that dragons were fast. He had also said that they were given to getting lost. If that were so, where might she be leading me? Still, I scampered along, not pausing until I reached a fork in the path. Which way had she gone? I listened, but heard nothing. Had she gone left? Had she gone right? Which should I choose? My decision was made for me when a terrible scream rent the air. It had come from down the right-leading trail. Then again. The same bloodcurdling cry!

I ran as quickly as I could, jumping over roots and fallen branches. There was a sudden clearing. It was lit by sun. I squinted at the unaccustomed brightness. My attention was caught by something dangling from a branch of a tree at the glade's edge. A banner? No. I looked closer. Of course! It was the dragon-skin wrap I had worn among the Trolavians. And lying on the ground directly beneath it, with her feet in the air, in what looked to be a dead faint, was Mary Jane. I ran towards her and heard a welcome voice.

"Goose!"

I looked up.

"Oh, Goose. Thank goodness it's you."

"Scally!"

He leaped from his branch and into my arms. I kissed the top of his head.

"Goose, Goose. We thought we'd lost you for good."

"We? But where is Belle?" I asked. As if in answer to my question, a shower of twigs drew my attention upwards. A familiar face, but a frightened one, peered down from between the leaves. And a familiar voice, quavering but still tuneful, sang out.

"Trouble, trouble, trouble! I am going to be in so much trouble!"

28

The Dragon Swoons

Take a dozen people, each of whom can paint equally well. Ask them to imagine a cake. Ask them to paint it. When they are done, you will have twelve very different cakes. Flat cakes. Layer cakes. Brown cakes. Pink cakes. Cake is a simple word, but no two people imagine "cake" in the same way. Or else, say "dragon." Right away, a picture comes to mind. But of what? Some see enormous purple lizards. Some see fire-breathing monsters. Some see snakes with wings. As sure as I am 101, the picture you hold in your head of the dragon Mary Jane is different from the picture that your sister or brother or best friend would conjure.

"Is it dead?" asked Belle, peering down from the tree.

"I don't think so," I answered, kneeling for a closer look.

The creature who lay before me was small. Soft. Not scaly, but spotted and covered with a fine fur.

"Don't wake it!" hissed Belle. "Who knows what it might do? I'm already going to be in such trouble with the magistrate for not having taken better care. I'll never make Corporal now. I'll probably get demoted to street cleaner, and Fergus and Bergus will never stop teasing me. And it'll be even worse if you go and get yourself killed by a dragon!"

"Don't be silly, Belle," I admonished. "This dragon is not going to hurt anyone."

"How can you be so sure?"

It was a good question. After all, I had no more personal experience of dragons than did Belle. Still, I was convinced that this was not a creature who was likely to misbehave. In the first place, I knew in my heart of hearts that anyone who could skip as well as Mary Jane could not be deeply evil. What was more, she had fainted, which did not suggest bloodthirstiness. I supposed that she must have been scared out of her wits by the sight of my wrap dangling from the tree.

"Believe me, Belle, she's even more frightened than you are. So you can come down from that tree."

"But I can't!"

"Of course you can. No one will harm you."

"I don't mean that I can't because I'm afraid. I am a soldier, after all. I mean that I can't because I *can't*. Trolavians were never designed for tree living. I'm stuck up here, just as the avalanche left me."

"She's quite right," said Scally. "Those long, skinny feet of hers are all wedged up among the branches. It's a terrible tangle. I don't see how we'll get her down without an axe."

"No! No axes. What if you miss the branch and hit my feet?"

"Do you have any better ideas?" asked Scally, tetchily.

"Calm down," I said, trying on a voice I hoped was authoritative.

"Very well for you to say calm down! No one is going to go after you with an axe!"

"We don't have an axe, Belle, so there's no need to worry."

Mary Jane moaned. She stirred. Scally yelped and jumped back up to a low branch.

"Look out!" shrieked Belle, who pulled her head back into the crown of branches.

"Hush. You'll only frighten her."

I knelt again beside the dragon.

"Mary Jane."

I held her by her dragon hand—it was surprisingly smooth and delicate—and shook it gently.

"Mary Jane. Wake up."

She opened her eyes. I watched her face register first bewilderment, then surprise, then alarm.

"Where am I? Where am I? And what are you?"

"My name is Penelope. I'm a visitor here. You fainted, Mary Jane."

"Mary Jane? Who is Mary Jane?"

Had I misheard her? Or had she hit her head when she fell? Did she no longer know herself?

"You're Mary Jane. Aren't you? That's the name you sang while you were skipping."

"I'm no more Mary Jane than I'm Polly-Put-the-Kettle-On. That was nothing more than a skipping rhyme! Do I look like a Mary Jane?"

"I don't know if you do or if you don't. I've never seen a dragon before. What is your name, then?"

"Quentin."

"Quentin?"

"Yes, Quentin! Are you deaf?"

Was I deaf? That was a question that would have taken much too long to answer.

"I'm just confused. Where I live, Quentin is a boy's name. Do you mean to say you're a boy dragon?"

"Of course I'm a boy dragon," he said, struggling to sit up. "If I weren't a boy dragon, I wouldn't be—"

But then he looked up into the tree. He saw again the dangling skin. His eyes widened, then rolled back in his head. And once again he collapsed in a deep, dead faint.

29

Taking Charge

I am Penelope. I am 101 years old. When people ask how I've managed to live so long, I answer that I have cultivated calmness of mind. I am untroubled by regret. I am sorry for nothing I have done. Nor do I pine for the things I've missed. And I can assure you I've missed a great deal. Why, I've never ridden a camel. I've never milked a yak. I've never smoked a pipe. What else? I've never learned to juggle, and I've never been to Paris, and I've never had tea with a duchess. I could write a very long catalog of things I've never done, but what would be the point? The world is full of magnificent possibilities, but even if you live to a very ripe old age you will never be able to explore them all. You must satisfy yourself with tasting as much as you can in the little time that you are given.

Regret will only wear you down. If ever I feel something like regret welling up, I need only remember that once in my life, if only in a dream, I did things to which no one else can lay claim. Once, I flew with a talking cat. Once, I revived a fainting dragon. When I remember that, even riding a camel pales in comparison.

You may have heard it said that an emergency will bring out either the best or the worst in people. As it happens, the same rule applies to cats and to Trolavians. Quentin's second fainting threw Belle into a panic, and Scally's good sense seemed to have been toppled by the avalanche. He could do nothing more than look down from his tree branch and mutter, "Oh, my stars and garters! Oh, my stars and garters!"

A calmness of mind. Was this the first time the prized calmness settled on me in a crisis? I think so. What is certain is that ever since that day in the dreamtime forest, I can be counted on to remain at ease when everyone around me is in a fretful flap. I would not call this a gift so much as a talent born of necessity. Maybe it was the shock of the avalanche. Maybe it was the sudden change of climate and the unaccustomed shine of sun. Whatever the reason, neither Scally nor Belle was in a position to be helpful when help was what was most required. There was no one else to turn to for assistance, no one else to make decisions. There was me, and me alone.

Do not think that by calmness I mean something passive and hazy. If this calmness had a color, it would not be minty green or misty blue, but a pure, hot white. It was not aimless. It was full of direction and purpose. Calmness came. My mind was clear.

"Scally!"

I was surprised by the ring of command in my own voice. Scally must have been as well. He stopped simpering and looked at me quizzically.

"Scally, listen to me. We have to do something about that dragon skin before Quentin wakes up. Can you hide it?"

He gave me a cattish grin and a nod.

"Hide the hide? Right you are!"

He took a corner in his jaws and hauled it up into the tree, where it was camouflaged by leaves.

"Belle," I said, with as much edge to my voice as I could muster, "I promise you, this dragon is not going to hurt you. When he wakes up I will need to talk to him. You must be quiet."

Scally sat beside her, and the two of them peered down from their high branch. I took the dragon by his hand. I gave him a gentle shake.

"Quentin. Wake up."

Again he stirred. Again he moaned. High in the tree I heard Belle gulp.

"Shhhhhhhhhh!" I warned, a finger to my lips. Quentin's eyelids were fluttering. For a moment I faltered. What if Belle was right? What if he was angry enough to want to harm me? But no. I could not let my mind stray in that direction. I unknotted the rope from around my waist. I measured its weight in my hands. I gave it an experimental turn or two. I satisfied myself that I had not lost my knack. And then I began to skip in earnest.

30

A Duel

Wake up, Quentin, wake up now.
Don't lie around like a silly old sow.
Quentin, Quentin, dare to skip.
I can jump a thousand and never ever slip.
With a ha ha ha and a hoo hoo hoo
I can skip a thousand times better than you!

It felt good to be skipping again. It felt good to hear that satisfying whack of the rope as it met the earth and to feel the soft forest floor beneath my feet. It felt good to feel my heart quicken, to breathe hard, to find that the words I needed were waiting on my tongue.

Jump! Your name is Quentin.
Jump! That's plain to see.
Jump! I know you'll never skip
Fast like me!

Quentin was coming to, and I wanted to be the first thing he saw when he shook off his faint. Slowly, slowly, he opened his eyes. He shook his head to clear away the cobwebs. He blinked hard, three times.

Jump! My name's Penelope.
Jump! I never rest.

Jump! As far as skipping goes
I'm the best.
Hop and leap and skip and jump.
Jump and leap and whirl.
There's no one can skip as well
As this girl!

I hadn't recognized that Quentin was a boy. Perhaps he didn't know that I was a girl, and it was vital to my plan that he understand this. If boy dragons were like boy humans, nothing would make one angrier than being challenged by a girl.

Hop and leap and skip and jump.
Jump and leap and whirl.
There's no one can skip as well
As this girl!

By the narrowing of his eyes and the pursing of his lips, I could see that I had struck a nerve. Quentin got to his feet, a little shakily at first. He steadied himself. He picked up his rope from where it had fallen. He curled his lip in a look of defiance. He began to skip.

Jump! My name is Quentin.
Jump! That's plain to see.
Jump! And there is no one who can
Skip like me.
Coal turns into diamonds.
Oysters give us pearls.

You're as slow as treacle and you're
Just a girl!

I called up all my flintiness. I gave him a look of withering contempt and picked up speed.

Hickory dickory bickery bock
Knickety rickety flippity flip.
Dragons are nothing but wind and talk,
I am the one who will win this skip!

Quentin was quick to answer.

Whickity whackity nickery nack
Singity songity pippety pop.
Yours is the rope that will soon go slack,
You are the one who will have to stop!

"Harpy, Harpy, Scarface!" That is what Mellon and the others call when they see me plodding down the road, bent over my cane. How is it possible that they don't know the truth of me? I have lived so long that I have outlasted my own legend.

"Hail, great dragon slayer!"

That is what they should properly say.

Well.

Perhaps not quite.

Not slayer.

Not slayer, exactly.

But close.

Quentin and I matched each other, turn for turn and skip for skip. When one of us would quicken the rhythm, the other would keep pace. Every cross-handed flourish was met with another. Every feat of fancy footwork was answered in kind. One of us would call out a challenge, and it would always be met.

"Kick skip!"

"One leg skip!"

"Double skip!"

I had never met so skilled and tireless an opponent, and I had skipped against the best Hamelin had to offer. Nan and Elfleda. Bridget and Newlyn. All the girls from up and down our lane. All girls who were in the hands of the Piper, and whom I had to find unless I wanted to spend the rest of my young life skipping alone. I quickened the tempo.

"Backward skip!"

"Turnaround skip!"

"Pepper skip!"

Neither of us could find a way to trip up the other. Our ropes hummed, and we skipped so fast that there was no rupture in the sound they made as they scuffed the earth. The forest rang with *whackitywhackitywhackitywhackity,* punctuated with the sound of our cries.

Jump! My name's Penelope.
Jump! I never rest.
Jump! As far as skipping goes
I'm the best!

Jump! My name is Quentin.
Jump! I can't be beat.
Jump! You're sure to finish up
In de - feat!

On and on we skipped, our ropes now nothing but blurs in the air.

"Shin cross skip!"

"Double jump back skip!"

"Spin around skip!"

"Click heels skip!"

"Ankle bend skip!"

Each was dispatched with equal aplomb.

"Give in," called Quentin. "You can't win against me. I can go forever."

"Forever?"

"And ever!"

"We'll see about that."

In a flash, I knew what I had to do.

"Somersault skip!"

He almost faltered.

"Somersault skip? No such thing."

"There is now!"

In all my skipping days I had never heard of such a maneuver, let alone attempted to bring it off. But I had to do this. If I could not best a dragon in a skipping contest, what chance would I have against the Piper?

"Go on!" panted Quentin. "I dare you!"

I put all my trust in my body. I left the ground. My head

and heels traded place, then traded place again. The rope never stopped its spinning as the world went topsy turvy. I was filled with joy. And I did it! I landed with a riotous whoop and saw with satisfaction that Quentin's jaw had dropped nearly to his knees.

"Your turn," I said, merrily.

"That was cheating!"

"Fraidy dragon!"

"Am not!"

"Then do it!"

His bulging eyes narrowed to tiny slits. He knew how much was riding on this.

"Somersault skip!" Quentin bellowed and up he flew, his every limb flailing, high, high, high into the air.

31

What Was Left of Machalus

If ever you have the chance to travel among the Trolavians, I recommend that you try the shortbread. Not only is it feather-light and flavorful, it is durable. So durable, in fact, that it can withstand the ravages of an avalanche and not even crumble. That is what I discovered when I opened Belle's picnic hamper, which the cascade of snow had sloughed off at the far edge of the clearing. The cookies and her flask of lemonade were still inside. I was glad to find them. Victory had left me feeling famished and thirsty.

"Eat this," I said to Quentin when he regained consciousness and I had unknotted the rope from around his arms and legs. I had propped him up against a mossy log. He was very pale. He shrank back from my offer of a cookie, and he looked so frightened that I couldn't keep from chuckling.

"Why are you laughing?"

"I'm sorry. It's just that all my life I've heard stories about dragons, and I never once supposed I'd meet one, and I never once supposed they'd be like you! Have some shortbread. It's delicious, I promise."

He looked at it suspiciously.

"It's green. How do I know it's not poisoned?"

"It's not poisoned."

"Prove it."

I bit into one of the cookies. I made a show of chewing deliberately and then swallowing. I licked the crumbs from my lips, and again offered the tin of treats. Slowly, slowly, he reached out and took one. He sniffed it, licked it, then swallowed it in one gulp.

"Why are you being so kind?"

"Because, Quentin, I have no reason to act otherwise. And because I don't know where I am. Because I am hoping you will answer some questions."

"But I must do anything you ask. That is dragon law. You bested me in a skipping contest. Now, I am your slave."

"Slave? No, no. I have no need of a slave, Quentin. I only need help."

"The law is the law and I must do your bidding, whatever it may be. But may I ask you one question?"

"Of course."

"Where did you learn such skipping?"

"I've always skipped. Until recently, it was the one thing I was good at. Where did *you* learn?"

"All dragons skip. We learn as soon as we can walk. Among dragons, skipping is an important sport. Why, there are songs and legends about our most famous skippers. Of course you have heard the Saga of Odo."

"No. Who was Odo?"

"Who was Odo? Why, only the greatest of all the great skippers. He was magnificent! A god! A somersault skip would have been child's play to Odo."

"Then among the dragons, both boys and girls skip?"

"Yes. We have tournaments. Only last week I won the Junior Grand Championship."

He sniffed. A tear made its way from his eye and down his long nose.

"I'd hoped that one day they would be singing the Saga of Quentin. But now I'll be lucky if I even get a ballad. I'll be lucky if I get a mere quatrain. Now, I've lost my title. Now, it belongs to you and I must be your servant."

"For goodness' sake! I don't want a servant, Quentin. I only want your help."

"A somersault skip. Who could have imagined such a thing? I should have known you were dangerous. I should have known when I saw poor Machalus hanging from the tree!"

"Machalus? Who's Machalus?"

"Don't pretend you don't know. That was Machalus I saw blowing in the breeze."

Of course. The dragon skin that had stopped him in his tracks.

"How can you be sure it was Machalus?"

"Every dragon knows every other dragon, and that is Machalus. Was Machalus, I mean. He was our famous pathfinder. The very best. He's been missing for years, and now I know what happened to him. You must have slain him, and you'll do the same to me!"

He was becoming quite overwrought.

"Please calm down, Quentin. I can explain. You see, your friend must have become lost—"

"To think I was nearly taken in by your show of kindness. Now I see it was all a ruse. Now I know you for who you are. A liar! A murderer!"

"Quentin! No! I'm—"

"Go ahead! Slay me! Skin me! That cookie *was* poisoned, wasn't it? It was all a trick! Oh, oh, oh! To die so young, and so ignoble a death!"

Once a troupe of traveling players had passed through Hamelin. One of the actors had performed a death scene that was so extravagant I fell into a fit of giggles. Now I did the same with Quentin.

"You can laugh," he declaimed, beating his breast. "It matters nothing to you that I'll never skip for the Piper!"

I snapped to attention. "The Piper?"

"The only way he'll ever see me now is as a blanket! I know it, I know it, I know it!"

And after spouting out a volley of sobs, he crumpled to the ground once again in a dead faint.

32

A Nice Little Way with Flowers

I am Penelope, and I regret nothing, as I have said. But that is not to say I would not rewrite the odd sentence in the story of my life, given the chance. For instance, I have a temper. On occasion, I have spoken sharply to somebody who did not deserve the cutting edge of my tongue. And even though I am proud of my workmanship, there are certain of my harps that I think might have been better crafted.

My many harps. I have been studying their virtues and their imperfections these last few days. I have been walking among them, tuning them carefully, trying to decide which should belong to the child. To Micah's daughter. Soon, he will bring her here. And when they come, I will tell them that if a harp is what young Penelope wants, a harp is what she shall have. It pleases me to think that the handiwork of one Penelope will pass into the keeping of another.

But I ramble. I get ahead of myself. They have not come yet. Not yet. Where was I? Where was I? Oh, yes. My temper. My harps. I also think I might have made an earlier start on this writing business. Now that I have a taste for it, I can see there is much more I could tell. For example, I could write a short treatise on what to expect if you meet a dragon. I could explain how to tell the male of the species from the female. He is spotted. She has a mane. I could tell you that dragons are prone to theatrical fits, but that these pass. I could tell you how to revive one when he faints.

"Quentin! Quentin, wake up."

"Dear Goose."

Scally had come down from his high perch.

"You were magnificent! Such virtuosity. Are you all right?"

"I'm fine, Scally. But we have to wake him. He knows about the Piper."

"A pity we didn't bring smelling salts. Perhaps a shortbread would do the trick?"

"Save some for me," Belle sang out from above, but she was doomed to disappointment. The last shortbread was sacrificed to wake the sleeping dragon. He opened his mouth to receive the tempting wafer. He heaved a dramatic sigh, then sat up.

"I'm not a blanket?"

"No," I said, firmly. "You are not a blanket, Quentin, and you are not my slave, either. But I am hoping you will help us. This is Scally, and our friend's name is Belle."

"Why is she hiding in that tree?"

"I'm not hiding," trilled Belle. "I happen to be stuck."

"We'll think of a way to get her down later. First, I will tell you who we are and why we're here. It will be hard to believe, but every word is true."

I sat cross-legged on the ground beside him. I took a deep breath. I began at the beginning. Harps and home. Rats and piping. Deafness and dreaming and falling and flying. All this I told him, as well as how the hide that was once the skin of Machalus had come into my possession and how the avalanche had swept us into the forest. How I had spotted Quentin from my high perch. How I had mistaken him for Mary Jane. How I had followed him along the path.

"And the rest you know. That is the how and the why of us."

He sat for a long, silent moment.

"It is asking a great deal of me to believe all this."

"But you must! It is true. All true. And now it is time for you to talk. You mentioned the Piper. How do you know him?"

"I don't. I know him only as a rumor. It's just that I was—"

"You were what?"

He swallowed hard. He sniffed back a tear.

"Oh, what does it matter if I tell you? My hopes are dashed anyway. I was running away from home."

"Quentin! Were you unhappy?"

"Unhappy and bored. Bored with home. Bored with my friends. Bored with being a dragon, really. You can't know what it's like, seeing only other dragons, playing only dragon games. It's nothing but skip and skip and skip and skip, and the occasional round of rummy. No music. No theater. No romance. Nothing for the soul."

"But the Piper is evil."

"What do I know about it? I've only heard that he is a wizard and that he lives in a palace and that he makes music. Think of it. A palace. Music. That is the life for which I was born."

"Careful, Goose," whispered Scally. "He's picking up steam. Any minute now he'll explode into another fainting fit."

"Quentin. Calm down. Breathe deeply."

He took a few deep gulps of air. He swallowed a swig of lemonade.

"Are there any more shortbreads?"

"All gone."

"Drat. They were tasty, even if the color was unsettling."

"Quentin. The Piper. What did you hope to do there?"

"Why, I'd hoped to find a position, of course."

"As what?"

"I could be his butler, perhaps. I could entertain him with fancy skipping. I could arrange flowers. Since he lives in a palace, there are bound to be flowers that need arranging."

"Flowers?"

"Oh, dear. I ought not to have said that. Father made me promise that I would never speak of it in public."

"Speak of what?"

"Flower arranging. It is very undragonly. Or so he says. But I can't help myself. I look at a bunch of flowers and I see so many possibilities. Their colors. Their shapes. I can't leave them alone. I have to arrange them into a lovely bouquet. I've always been that way, ever since I was a tiny dragonette. Nature has never been enough for me. I always feel it can be improved through Art."

"I'm not sure I understand."

"I'll show you. Wait here."

Quentin scurried about the clearing, quickly gathering up a fistful of lavender, black-eyed daisies, bluebells, and tiny wild roses. He stuck them haphazardly into the flask of lemonade. I caught a small squawk of protest from Belle up in her tree.

"I'd rather a crystal vase, but this will have to do. Now, watch carefully."

I expected that he would fuss with the flowers as I had seen Ebba do, but he stood back from the cluster and looked at it, long and deep. He released a loud sigh, and the blooms began to move of their own accord, pink against white against blue. Blue and white against pink. Pink and blue against white. It was like watching a kaleidoscope shift from one pretty pattern to another. Finally, the flowers seemed to agree on an arrangement that satisfied all their needs. They settled into stillness.

"There!" said Quentin.

"Astonishing," said Scally.

"I've never seen anything like it," I agreed.

"Oh, that's nothing. I can do much more than that. That tree, for instance," he said, pointing to where Belle was still stuck. "See how tightly those branches are clustered? Don't you think it would be nicer if they were better spaced? Watch."

Again, the look of concentration came over his face. Again, he let go of a long sigh. The tree seemed to relax. There was a shaking in the crown. The leaves trembled. The branches began to move, like fingers releasing a fist to reveal an open palm. The shade parted. A new beam of sunlight shone through. There was loud rustling, then a snapping of twigs and a flapping of wings and a musical squawk as Belle was released from her prison of branches and tumbled down to join us.

33

Now We Are Four

"Do you know what, Goose?"

"What?"

"I think you're terribly brave."

I held him tight. "I think you are, too."

Scally and I had to raise our voices against the whistle of the wind, for once again we were airborne. We were held aloft by the unfailing beat of Belle's wide wings. She seemed indefatigable. The exertions of the journey; the bruises raised by the avalanche and her fall from the tree: none of these dampened her spirits or slowed her in the slightest. She was just as strong and as steady as she had been when we left the Valley of the Singing Trolavians. Nor did she seem weighed down by the extra encumbrance of a sleeping dragon. At first I had wondered if she would agree to have Quentin as a passenger, for while he had jumped at the chance to join our party, Belle had bristled at the suggestion.

"Come with you to find the Piper? I should say so!" he enthused when I extended the invitation. "I was on my way there anyway, and I imagine you'll be needing me."

"No doubt," muttered Belle. "I'm sure we'll find he has some flowers in desperate need of arranging. You can look after those while we rescue the children."

"Was that snide?" asked Quentin.

"If snide is what you deserve, snide is what you'll get," Belle spat back.

Centuries of suspicion had grown up between Trolavians and dragons. Trolavians thought dragons were dim. Dragons thought Trolavians were murderers. This enmity would have to be set aside if we were to have any chance of success.

"Stop!" I said, and stepped between them. "Stop right now!"

I was surprised that they did as I said, and even more surprised to hear what sounded like Ebba's voice coming out of my mouth. Hadn't she often upbraided Sophy and me with these same words?

"I never want to hear another angry remark from either of you. We have to work together, and we can't have any of this silly bickering."

They both looked at the ground.

"Now, I want you each to say one nice thing about the other. Quentin, you first."

"Must I?"

"Yes."

He winced.

"Fine, then. Belle, I think you have a very nice voice."

Belle gave me a sidelong glance. I looked at her sternly. She grimaced.

"And I think it's very nice that you don't breathe fire."

Quentin looked at her, astonished.

"Is that supposed to be a compliment?"

"It was the best I could manage. I'd always thought that dragons breathe fire, and I'm very glad you don't. It would make me nervous if you did."

"Who told you dragons breathe fire? I've never heard such nonsense."

"I'd heard that as well," said Scally. "I think it's a widely held belief."

"Poppycock!"

And they might have gone on and on in such a way had I not called for calm.

"Perhaps we can discuss all this another time. We have to move on. Belle, are you able to carry the three of us?"

"Easily."

"This isn't Trolavian weather. You won't overheat?"

"No, no. I'm actually finding this warmer climate quite agreeable."

"And Quentin, can you tell me in which direction we should travel to find the Piper?"

"We go directly east."

"Due west, then," muttered Belle, and I remembered what the Magistrate had said about dragons and their flawed sense of direction.

"What was that?" asked Quentin, hackles on the rise.

"Remember our agreement, Belle," I warned. She made a show of protesting her innocence.

"I know, I know. I only said, 'You rest, then.' You've had quite enough excitement for today, Quentin. So, you rest, and I'll fly."

That seemed to sit well with our new companion, and Belle managed to be gracious when he offered his services as navigator.

"How kind. I'll be sure to call on you if I need your assistance."

Happily, Quentin was busy gathering up his flowers and

his skipping rope and so did not see her roll her eyes.

"Goose."

"Yes, Scally."

"We do have one small obstacle to overcome."

"What is that?"

"How will Belle carry us? The basket was smashed to bits by the avalanche, and I don't think we could all three travel on her back."

This knocked the stuffing right out of me. We had come so far. We were within sight of our goal. And now, it looked as if our mission might fail. I sat on a log and held my head in my hands. I fought back the tears. A chill wind made its way between the thick trunks of the trees. I shivered—all of a sudden I had my answer.

"Of course!"

"Goose?"

"Scally, fetch down Machalus, will you?"

He scaled the tree, disappeared into the branches, and re-emerged moments later with the dragon hide in his jaws.

"Oh, dear," Quentin moaned.

"I know this must be difficult," I said, as reassuringly as I could. "But there's no other way. The skin is strong. It's stretchy. It's all we have. And we have no more time to waste."

I tied my skipping rope around my waist. Quentin watched uneasily while Scally and Belle worked on fashioning a sling and knotting it firmly onto her long Trolavian feet.

"It's quite comfy," said Scally, who was first aboard. I climbed in to join him. Poor Quentin held back, tentatively fingering the skin of his countryman.

"Quentin, if you're coming with us, you have to come now."

Belle flapped her wings to signal her readiness. Finally, Quentin shrugged, sighed, and clambered in.

"Everyone comfortable?" asked Belle. "Then hang on. We're off to find the Piper."

34

Over the Hills and Far Away

No doubt there are, somewhere, dragons who spit fire. And it's almost certain that there are also winged dragons who fly through the air. Not Quentin. He was as distressed at finding himself airborne as he had been at the suggestion that flames might erupt from his mouth.

"Oh my goodness!" he'd exclaimed as we left the ground behind and flew straight up above the trees.

"Dear, dear," said Scally. "He doesn't look at all well."

And it was true that Quentin had gone quite green around the rims of his eyes.

"Oh my goodness!" said the dragon for a second time. He leaned over the edge of the skin and was loudly and copiously sick.

"I'd rather he breathed fire," chuckled Scally.

"Waste of good shortbread," sang out Belle.

Now Quentin slept, exhausted by the events of the day. Scally cuddled close and closed his eyes. I was glad of his warmth, and glad to have some peace as we flew above a country altogether different from the snowbound hills of the

Trolavians. I watched forest give way to rock and scrub, and rock and scrub give way to verdant, rolling plains punctuated by rivers and ponds. So tranquil. The view went on for miles and miles. I could see nothing that looked like danger. But danger was there, somewhere. I knew that danger was surely there, and we were flying towards it.

Dangerous.

I remembered how I had read the word on Ebba's lips.

Dangerous.

As we flew towards the setting sun, into the growing darkness, I felt something like fear wrap its fingers around my heart. I pried it loose. I could not let it take me over. I made myself remember the children so that I would not lose sight of my purpose. Sophy with her lovely voice and her sweet, sweet nature. Dogmael, who could do handstands and turn eight cartwheels in a row and never come up dizzy, and quiet Hildelith, who could work out complicated division problems in her head. Clever Simon, who always knew where the trout were biting.

I looked down on the earth, looked down on its dusky, rounded edges and thought of Ludwan, who was good at games. Bernard, whose thumb was so green he could grow potatoes in the sand. Ambrose, who could draw anything. I remembered Sezni, who wrote beautiful poetry, and her brother Ogilvie, who forgot to breathe when he was born and who was given up for dead until he suddenly gulped for air.

And as we flew through the thick of night, flew through a moonless sky, I remembered my parents, Ebba and Govan. It hurt me, knowing that they were sitting by the bedside of the other Penelope. I thought of how helpless they must feel, relying on one daughter, who was asleep, to find their other daughter, who was lost. It was no less difficult to think of Alloway, to guess at his desolation and loneliness. Poor Alloway! The only child in Hamelin. The only one left behind.

What I wouldn't have given to have had Alloway with us as we flew towards the Piper. His familiar, reassuring voice. His good humor. His wicked mimicry. What fun he would have had impersonating Belle and Quentin. And it must be said that, although I enjoyed being in the company of a cat, a Trolavian, and a dragon, I was beginning to hanker after human contact.

All night we flew, into the west, into the wind. All night we flew above the invisible earth, and one mile turned into ten turned into a hundred. I could not say exactly how far we traveled, but by the time the sun edged over the horizon I could see that we had left the land long behind. Now we were coursing along above gray and choppy water, with no shoreline in sight.

"Good heavens," said Quentin, when he finally came to. "Aren't we there yet?"

"Wherever in the world 'there' might be," yawned Scally.

"How are you faring, Quentin?" I asked.

"Much better, thank you."

"Did you have sweet dreams?"

"I dreamed of Machalus, in fact," he answered, venturing a peek over the side. "You know, the truth is that I never liked him very much. He was a terrible blowhard, and not nearly the pathfinder he claimed to be. There's even a skipping song about him.

Flickery flackery shoes and socks
Machalus stepped in an open box.
Knickery knackery spoons and spouts
Once inside he couldn't get out!
Poor old Machalus, wander he would,
Poor old Machalus, lost for good!

"Land ho!" called Belle, and we all three looked out and down and into the distance. There, far beneath us, lashed by the wind-riled water, was what I at first took to be a small island, narrow and round, with a pebbly beach surrounding a craggy pinnacle. The pinnacle reared up out of the waves, like a single, bony finger raised in admonition. As we circled down and down, closer and closer, I saw that the conical rise was pocked here and there by holes.

"Like windows," said Scally. "But what kind of a rock has windows?"

"No ordinary rock, that's certain," I answered, for I had begun to suspect the truth of what it was—a fortress, cleverly carved out of a strange, narrow heft of rock face. There could hardly be a better place for a prison. Which, I now believed, was surely what this was. And I didn't doubt for a moment who we would find locked up inside.

"I believe, my friends," I said, "that we have arrived."

And as if in answer, a pennant raised by some unseen hand slithered up a flagpole. It caught the wind and unfurled, flapping in the stiff breeze. It was emblazoned with a crest composed of a flute and a grinning red-eyed rat.

"And it looks," said Scally, "as if the Piper is at home."

35

The Bestowing of Alloway

Nothing happens without a reason. Those were Cuthbert's words from long ago. I have never forgotten them. In all my 101 years, I have never doubted that they are true. However, it must be said that some reasons are harder to find than others. What, I wonder, is the reason for Mellon? What purpose does he serve, other than to prove that there is such a thing as brutishness in the world? If one day he were to simply disappear, would Earth be the poorer? If one day he were to be turned into a rat, say, would anyone really miss him? I am tempted to test it, I can tell you. It would require only a very few words to give him four legs and a tail. But I mustn't. I promised myself I wouldn't, and I mustn't. Mustn't. Mustn't.

Many people who live alone talk to themselves. I long ago acquired the habit, and I sometimes forget that I am speaking my thoughts out loud. Only this afternoon I was repeating the word "mustn't" when I saw a familiar figure in my doorway.

"Micah."

"Do you have company, Penelope? I heard you talking."

"Muttering to myself. Come in."

"I have brought someone to meet you."

But whoever it was was hanging back, out of view.

"She is shy," Micah explained. He reached out, and a hand reached back to touch his. Your hand, Penelope. The first thing I saw of you was your hand. Micah drew you to his side. You clung to him.

"Penelope," he said. "Enough."

You burrowed into his cloak.

"Enough! You are soon to be eleven. That's too old for playing such timid games."

You summoned courage. You came out of hiding. You looked at me long. Quizzically. You sent me a shy smile. You stood in plain view, and I saw you for the first time.

"Come here."

You came. I watched as you studied my marred face. The mended tear on my cheek.

"Give me your hands."

Such thin, long fingers. Perfect for the harp. I held them in my own gnarled fists. I could feel the beating of your pulse. I could feel the life coursing through you. I felt as if I'd always known you.

"You are Penelope," I said.

"Yes."

"And I am Penelope, too."

Penelope. The name was out of fashion even when I was a girl. In all my 101 years, I had never met another Penelope. I am glad to know one now. It pleases me to write the word "Penelope" and have it call to mind someone with a face other than my own. A young face. One that is as yet unscarred. And it pleases me to know that it is another Penelope who will take charge of Alloway. For that is the name of your harp. The harp I chose for you. I offered it as a gift.

"You cannot simply give it to her, Penelope. You must let me pay you."

"No, Micah. I have decided. When is her birthday?"

"Exactly a week from now."

"Good. Penelope, you and your father must return to see me in a week less a day. Come again on your elevening eve. Then your harp will be ready for you."

Alloway. It is not the best of the lot, but it is the one I love above all others. I am glad that you shall have it. It was the second harp I ever made. And now, I will tell you the story of the first. Now, I shall take you to meet the Piper.

Section v

playing for the piper

36

A Wishing Skip

Belle came to roost on the narrow ring of beach that circled the base of the Piper's island fortress. Happily, we managed to land there undetected; or so it seemed. There was no sign of anything like a guard house or sentry post, perhaps because none was needed. The cliff soared above us with no ledge or foothold, making the fortress completely inaccessible from the ground.

"Now what do we do, Goose?" asked Scally, after we had disembarked and assessed the situation.

I tried to muster some of the "take charge" bravado I had known in the forest.

"Now we meet the Piper," I said.

"How will we get in?" asked Quentin.

"Belle, can you fly us to the top?"

"Easily," she said, "but once we're there, how do we explain ourselves?"

It was a good question. This was not the sort of place where visitors turned up unannounced or neighbors dropped by for tea. We would need a plan, and luckily, thanks to Quentin, I had one. All his hand-wringing and breast-beating early on had put me in mind of the theatrical troupes that sometimes came through Hamelin, wandering actors and minstrels and tumblers who performed songs and poetic recitations and juggling acts. These always drew an appreciative audience of townsfolk who were happy to part with a coin or two in exchange for some relief from the boredom of everyday life. As a very young man, Govan had spent a happy year with just such a company, meandering about the countryside, playing his harp and singing his songs. Now in her own way, his daughter was going to follow in his footsteps.

"My friends," I announced to my brave companions, "I am pleased to welcome you into the celebrated ranks of the Deep Dream Traveling Players."

"I beg your pardon?" asked Belle.

"The Deep Dream Traveling Players. We wander the world putting on theatrical entertainments. In exchange for nothing more than food and lodging, we present a memorable evening of song, dance and poetry. And that," I said, gesturing to the Piper's castle, "is where we will mount our next show."

"Goose!" said Scally. "You amaze me!"

"And once we're inside," I continued, "we'll find Sophy and the others."

I tossed this off with glib assurance, as though it would be as simple as asking the time of day. Belle and Quentin, however, were not so easily convinced.

"But wait," said Belle. "Even if we do get inside, and even if we do find the children, do you suppose the Piper will simply turn them over to us?"

"We'll find a way to free them," I answered. I tried to sound sure of myself, but in truth I was feeling less and less confident all the time.

"And how do we know that he'll even agree to see us?" asked Quentin. "What if he just slams the door in our faces?"

"Surely he'll be glad to see us," I answered, hoping to

convince myself. "After all, theatrical entertainments must be a rare thing around here."

"But what will happen when we have to perform? He's sure to find out that we're frauds."

"Oh, come, Belle," said Scally, taking up the cause. "Think of how much talent we have among us! You can sing. And as for Quentin, well, he could—"

"Arrange flowers!" sang Belle.

"Yes. Or I could recite one of the dragon sagas," volunteered Quentin. "They go on for hours and hours."

"I suppose if there are any rats around, I could catch them," Scally offered with a mischievous grin. "I'm a little out of practice, but I don't think I've lost my touch altogether."

"No, Scally," I countered. "You must be our Master of Ceremonies. You can introduce each of the acts."

"But Penelope," asked Belle, practical as always, "what about you? Won't the Piper lock you up with all the rest? The Magistrate will have my hide if you wind up in that prison!"

"What did you say, Belle?" I asked.

"I said the Magistrate will have my hide."

"Of course!"

"Of course what?"

"The hide. Machalus is the answer. I could wear his hide and disguise myself as a dragon. If only I had some way to stitch it up!"

By the time this writing passes into your keeping, Penelope, you will be eleven. The day will come, sooner rather than later, that you will begin your own adventures. And when that day arrives, it might well be that you cross paths with a dragon. Such things happen, and I ought to know. You will not have met a dragon before, of course, but it won't matter. I feel sure that you will know him for what he is. Or her. Meeting a dragon is like falling in love. Even though you have never experienced it before, you will know when it has happened.

Now, should you meet a dragon, and should you not know what to say after saying hello, you can always ask him what he carries in his pouch. Every dragon, whether boy or girl, has a pouch at his middle, much like a kangaroo. Kangaroos have pouches so that they can carry their young. Dragons use them to store important things. Their treasures. Quentin, as it turned out, carried in his Scotch mints, a compact mirror and a sewing kit.

"It was my Gran's," he explained when he brought out the kit. "She always said you could never tell when it would come in handy. I guess she was right. Hold still. I'll stitch you up. By the time I'm through, you'll look like a proper dragon."

Quentin proved himself a fast and expert tailor. "There!" he exclaimed, smacking on a Scotch mint as he put the final stitches in my disguise. "You look more like Machalus than Machalus himself."

"Very nice job," said Scally. "Quite seamless."

"It's nothing, really," he blushed.

"Bravo!" said Belle. "But what will Penelope do to entertain the Piper?"

Scally answered in his best Master of Ceremonies voice.

"Ladies and Gentlemen. We come now to our Grand Finale. Our next act has thrilled audiences in London and Paris. In Rome and Cologne. They are arch rivals in the dangerous art of Rope Jumping. Tonight, they have vowed to skip to the death to determine who is the Consummate Skipper. The Deep Dream Traveling Players are proud to present—Quentin and Fenton. The Dueling Dragon Duo!"

"How thrilling," Belle chirped.

"Yes," said Quentin, "and I can't wait to give that somersault skip another try."

By the time our plans were laid, the sun was sinking low on the horizon. We agreed to spend the night on the beach and present ourselves to the Piper in the morning. Belle had wisely pointed out that we would be needing a carrier basket, now that I was wearing Machalus on my back. She set off with Scally and Quentin in search of enough reeds and sticks to make one.

"It's a pity we don't have Sophy here to weave it," said Scally, "but I've seen her do it a hundred times or more. I think we can make something serviceable."

I waved good-bye as they started down the beach. I was glad to have some time to myself. I had to get accustomed to skipping in my dragon getup. I took my rope and began to turn.

Clouds turn into rainstorms, oceans turn to foam,
Count aloud the years since you've been home.
Scissors, rocks and paper, needles, threads and pins,
Think of who you're missing and then call him in!
Ladle, spoon and saucepan, kettle, steam and spout,
Choose the one you'd like to see and shout it out!

And so on the beach, I skipped and called their names. Ulfrid and Richard. Kea and Radegun. Brigid and Maura and Cannice and Joan. Henry and Sophy and Theo and Roan. One after one, I named the children of Hamelin. And with each name I made a vow that somehow I would find a way to bring them back to their families. Chantal. Gregory. Margaret. Had I thought of everyone? No. No. Someone had been left out. He was not missing like the others. But he was absent in his own way, and I felt his loss as keenly. I called up his face. I called out his name.

Scissors, rocks and paper, needles, threads and pins,
Alloway, Alloway, now come in!

All of a sudden my rope was knotted in tangles and I was tripping over my new dragon feet. For where just a moment before there had been nothing but empty air, there he stood. Alloway. Somehow, he had heard me. Somehow, he had come. And he had not come alone. At his side was Ulysses, grinning a silly, doggy grin, wagging his tail, old but sturdy on his three long legs.

37

My First Harp

Three days have passed, Penelope, since I wrote those last words. I have spent the time between then and now in bed. I don't know how to name the illness that settled on me. A heaviness in my heart. A burning in my lungs. As though I had been walking for a very long time up a very steep hill. I drifted the whole time between sleep and wakefulness.

Such strange dreams. Cuthbert was in them, along with Alloway and Sophy. Ebba was there. So was Govan, and he had his harp. How beautifully he played! Quentin and Belle were there. Yet whenever I opened my eyes, whenever I left my dreams, it was the Shadow who was with me. It lay on my chest, just as Scally did when I was a girl. But while Scally was soft and warm, the Shadow was a chilling presence. It spoke to me. Whispered sweet nothings. It wanted to stay and press itself on me, even when I felt well enough to rise.

"Be gone, Shadow. I have much to do!"

And finally, it heeded my remonstrations. Finally, it left me alone. Now, no more dilly dallying! I must make haste. Your elevening eve comes in two more days. Then Micah will bring you to fetch your harp. In just two more days you will come for Alloway, and I still have much to prepare. I still have more to tell.

Scissors, rocks and paper, needles, threads and pins,
Alloway, Alloway, now come in!

And he was there, along with three-legged Ulysses. I whooped with happy surprise. I completely forgot that I was wrapped in the skin of Machalus. That poor dog! Scooped up out of his accustomed time and place only to find a dragon running towards him, he bayed a warning.

"Ulysses!" called Alloway. "What on—"

But before he could finish, I had tackled him.

"You've come! You've come!" I shouted, and we three tumbled about on the stony strand, a happy tangle of eleven limbs. Never has there been a more joyous reunion than the one we had on that shore.

"What has happened to you, Penelope?" he asked, running his hands over my dragon face. "Your skin!"

"Oh, Alloway. That is a long, long story. You tell me first. How did you get here?"

"I can't say. I was exhausted by so much sadness. The missing children. Their sobbing parents. Ebba and Govan, silent and distraught at your bedside. I went to the stable. I lay down in the straw. Ulysses stretched out beside me. He has been my constant companion ever since he found me in the forest. Cuthbert says he wants to be sure I don't wander off again."

"He is a true and loyal friend to have followed you this far."

"But how far is 'this far'? Where am I, Penelope?"

And so we sat and so we talked, and I told him of everything I'd seen and done since I began my Deep Dream wanderings. If Alloway, blind since birth, was disappointed not to have been given sight in this other place, as I had regained my hearing, he didn't say so. He talked only of finding the children.

"Are you certain Sophy and the others are locked up inside the fortress?"

"I feel it in my bones, but the only way to know for sure is to get inside."

"Yes. We must. We must."

How he loved Sophy! My heart ached to see it. His longing alone should have been strong enough to free her. On and on we talked, and when the others returned with their bundles of sticks, you can imagine how astonished they were to find us.

"Dear Goose," said Scally, leaping up to my shoulder. "Alloway is a pleasant surprise, but was it really necessary to import that dog along with him?"

"It's a pity Alloway doesn't have his harp," said Quentin. "We could make him a part of our traveling company. He could play for the Piper."

"I could build him one," I said. I felt a tingling excitement surge through me as I said the words.

"Could you, Goose?"

"Yes. If only we had the materials, I could build him one myself."

And with that assertion, I claimed my future.

"Do you still have the necklace I gave you, Penelope?" asked Alloway.

I touched my throat and felt the eight braided strings. A silent octave. I had become so accustomed to the feeling of it on my skin that I had forgotten it was there.

"Yes."

"If we have the strings, then we're halfway to a harp."

"We saw some driftwood on the beach," volunteered Belle.

"Driftwood? Oh, I don't think—"

But I stopped short. I remembered Govan saying that a harp could be wrought from any wood. The maker's work was to listen to it. Listen for the beating of its heart. Listen for the song that lived in the grain.

"I'll fetch it," said Belle, and off she flew.

And that, Penelope, was the beginning of what became the rest of my life. I took the wood Belle brought. I held it. I listened. I heard. And I began. With what I had around my neck and with beach-found scraps of wood lashed together with reeds, I made my first harp. It was not a pretty thing, but it was true to its purpose. I finished. I asked it to sing. I gave it to Alloway. He played. And sing it did. It sang, Penelope. How it sang!

38

The piper speaks

It is a pity, Penelope, that you will never have the chance to learn about your new instrument from Govan, for there was never a better harper than my father. There was never a better teacher. Govan taught his pupils that music is more than melody. More than hitting the right notes. He taught them that an open heart is just as important to music-making as are nimble fingers.

"You must never forget," he would tell his apprentices, "that music is a sacred trust. Of all God's gifts, it is the greatest. You must always have respect. Respect for the music. Respect for your gift and for your instrument. Respect for your audience. It does not matter if you play for a king or a beggar, for one person or for a thousand. You must always bring to your harping the same qualities of attention and love. It is God's gift you carry in your hands. Respect it. Burnish it. Give it back again."

Govan was a man of high ideals, Penelope. He practiced what he preached. But even he would have had a hard time summoning respect for the audience that assembled to watch the first and last performance of the Deep Dream Traveling Players.

"Hang on!" cried Belle, as she lifted us straight into the air and up the vertical rise of the fortress tower. We circled around it, searching for some way in. There was no obvious entrance, no ladder or stairs that led to anything like a portal. Finally, we passed a door made of thick wooden planks and decorated with an impressive iron knocker, cast in the shape of a wedge of cheese.

"Brie, if I'm not mistaken," said Scally.

Belle hovered before it, like a hummingbird at a blossom, while Quentin reached out to grab the knocker. He hammered loudly, three times, then three times again. Finally, we heard a muttering and a scrabbling on the other side. The door swung open, and a huge rat, dressed in a tattered uniform, squinted out at us.

"What the devil is this?" he snarled. He could be forgiven for being puzzled. We must have been a very strange sight. A huffing Trolavian, dangling a makeshift basket containing two dragons, a cat, a three-legged dog and a boy carrying a driftwood harp. He laughed when we told him why we had come.

"A little play, is it? Ha! Well, the Master don't take kindly to visitors," snarled the rat, whose teeth were bad and whose breath was worse. "But wait here. He might like to have a gander at you. I've never seen the like myself."

He entered the fortress. A few minutes later, he returned.

"Your lucky day," he sneered. "Seems the Master thinks that a frolic might be good for the troops. Raise morale, he said. Whatever that is. He asked if you were funny. You're funny-looking, that's for sure. But are you funny?"

"Hilarious," answered Scally. "In Madrid they were rolling in the aisles."

"I don't know Madrid from a hole in the wall. You're a cat, ain't ya?"

"Why, yes. Very astute of you to notice."

"We don't like cats around here," he hissed, brandishing his lance.

"Oh, goodness. You have nothing to fear from me. I've reformed."

"I don't know nothing about no reform. All I know is that you better be funny. And there better be no funny business, either. If you know what I mean."

"Indeed, I do, good sir. Indeed I do."

We were escorted to a large, windowless assembly hall and instructed to wait. The cavernous room was lit by smoky torches. There was a platform at one end, which would serve as a stage, and a great many benches to accommodate the members of our audience.

"Not much of a theater, is it?" remarked Quentin.

"Terrible acoustics," added Belle, after she had sung an experimental scale.

"We'll just have to make do," I said, trying to sound optimistic. Alloway felt for my dragon skin–wrapped hand and gave it a squeeze.

"Don't worry," he said. "We'll be out of here before you know it. We'll be out of here and home."

While I was glad he was so encouraging, I was beginning to wonder about the wisdom of my plan. Foolhardy or not, though, we no longer had any choice but to proceed. Word of our arrival must have spread quickly throughout the fortress, because within minutes the place was jammed with an eager audience. I saw no sign of Sophy or any of the others. Nor did I see the Piper. But from the inside of my dragon costume, I looked out upon a sight familiar from the world of the waking. I cannot say I was happy to see it. Nor was Scally. In fact, he was aghast.

"Oh, Goose. It is bad enough that I must share the stage with a dog. But it is a thousand times worse that I should be reduced to glad-handing before a crowd of rats. The smell of them, Goose! The noise! If we were at home, I would unsheathe my claws right now and wreak a bit of havoc."

It was certainly a crowd that might have benefited from some discipline, for gathered in the hall around us, hooting and shouting and carrying on, was an assembly of rats every bit as raucous and rude as the rats that had once run roughshod over Hamelin. Indeed, it is possible they might have been those very rats. Some waved to their friends across the room. Some thumbed their noses and shouted insults. Some spat and swore. All of them hurled bits of rotting fruit and stale buns at one another, and at us.

"Showtime! Showtime! Showtime!" they bellowed, stomping their feet on the benches.

Scally did his best to quell the din. Obviously, he had paid close attention to the opening palaver delivered by the actors attached to the wandering troupes that had passed through Hamelin. No one could have guessed it was Scally's first time on the stage.

"We humble thespians bid you welcome, each and every one. The Deep Dream Traveling Players are honored to be among you. We have orchestrated, for your delectation and edification, a modest but pleasing spectacle of music and acrobatic panache."

"Keep your panache!" cried one of the rats.

"Stow your acrobatics!" bellowed another.

"Bring on the three-legged dog!" hollered a third.

"The three-legged dog! The three-legged dog!" they clamored in chorus.

We watched them anxiously from our places on the shabby stage.

"What do we do now?" asked Belle, nervously.

"I'm not sure," I answered, feeling all my confidence drain away.

"I've never seen such rudeness," said Quentin.

Scally tried bravely to press on.

"What good sports you are," he shouted, hardly able to make himself heard. "Why, we've rarely in all our travels had the chance to entertain so responsive an audience. How many of you are fond of singing?"

A great chorus of boos rose up from the rats.

"Lovely singing, of course, from that Mistress of Moonlight and Melody, Belle, the Trolavian."

Now he was pelted with banana skins and apple cores.

"Of course," Scally continued, gamely dodging these missiles, "singing may not be your cup of tea, but I know how thrilled you will be as the Deep Dream Traveling Players present those arch jump rope rivals, Quentin and Fenton. Please welcome the Dueling Dragon Duo!"

But they wanted nothing of it. A near riot broke out as the spectators clapped their ratty hands and stamped their ratty feet and sang out in rhythmic chorus:

"No! No! No! The three-legged dog! No! No! No! Bring on the dog!"

Ulysses whined and pressed his damp nose against my neck. I tried desperately to think of what he might do. Sit and beg? Roll over? Bark out "Twinkle Twinkle"? We had not planned that he would perform, yet now he was the one the rats wanted to see.

"The three-legged dog! The three-legged dog! Make the dog dance! Make the dog dance!"

"Silence."

A voice came from the back of the hall.

"Silence."

One word that cut straight through the brouhaha of the rioting rats. That *"silence"* was like a finely tempered sword that severed every tongue. The rats stood and turned. They bowed low. They parted ranks. And the man we had come so far to see strode between them.

Piebald hat and piebald tunic. Piebald stockings and

piebald cloak. The thin and jagged face. The cruel mouth and gleaming eyes. He was much as I remembered him from that afternoon in April, when he had stood in the town square and raised his pipe to his lips and set the rats to dancing. But then, he had seemed almost transparent. Here in the world of Deep Dreaming, where he had made his home for so many years, he pulsed and crackled.

"Enough of this foolishness."

He strode to the front of the hall, and every eye followed him. In that dim room, he seemed somehow to shine, but with dark purpose.

"Enough of this nonsense. Bring forth the blind harper."

Every eye turned towards the only one among us who had no eyes to see. Everyone turned towards Alloway.

"Bring forth the blind harper and I will hear him play. And let's invite our little songbird to sing, too."

"Goose!" said Scally, and I swallowed my impulse to jump from the stage. For behind the Piper came a retinue of rats. The rats hauled behind them a creaking cart. On the cart was a gilded cage. And in the cage was Sophy.

39

The Song of the Thrush

Poor Sophy! I have never seen anyone look as disconsolate as my sister did when she was wheeled into that rat-jammed hall. She kept her head lowered and did not look towards us. As for Alloway, he had no notion of the cage or of who was in it.

"And tell me, my pretty one," said the Piper, with a leer that made me shiver, "what will you sing for us?"

She mumbled.

"Speak up!"

She whispered again.

" 'The Song of the Thrush,' " crowed the Piper. "Delightful. Harper! My little bird has said that she will sing 'The Song of the Thrush.' Do you know it?"

Alloway nodded. Quentin led him to the front of the stage. Ulysses followed and lay down beside him, looking out on the crowd with baleful eyes. Alloway plucked a chord or two on his new harp. He began to play.

One day, Penelope, you will be a very fine musician. I would not give you my favorite among all my harps if I did not believe that it would be so. The day will come when your touch upon the instrument will be as much a part of you as the whorls upon your fingertips. It will be your signature.

Alloway was not a great harp player, but Govan had taught him well. He too had a touch that was his own, and Sophy knew it straight away. I watched recognition register on her face as he played the opening notes. She lifted her head. She looked down from her cage. She saw her harpist. She swallowed a gasp of astonishment. He reached the measure where she ought to have come in, but surprise had made her mute.

"Wake up, little bird," sneered the Piper. "We are all anxious to hear you sing."

Alloway began again, and this time, she sang. She was hesitant at first, but she warmed to the task.

And now it was Alloway's turn to be shocked, for just as she knew his harper's touch, so he knew her unmistakable voice.

Now has come the evening
When all God's creatures rest.
Now has come a mother thrush
Returning to her nest.

I held my breath. I willed him not to falter.

Now has come a mother thrush
To find her babies gone.
All her pretty feathered ones
Have taken wing and flown.

I had grown up with music. Troubadours from all over the world had come to Hamelin to pay homage to Govan in his prime. I had heard many remarkable players and singers. But I can tell you, Penelope, there had been nothing that could equal this.

With every word, Sophy's voice grew clearer. With every note, Alloway's playing grew more confident. To hear the two of them spin such sweet harmonies was like listening to a pledge of love. Even the rats forgot to be rats. They listened, enchanted.

All her pretty feathered ones
Have taken to the sky.

My heart is broken, cries the thrush,
I fear that I may die.
She sings her last, most mournful song.
It echoes far and near.
Then tucks her head beneath her wing
And sheds a final tear.

The last note rang on and on. Then there was nothing but quiet. Sophy stared down at Alloway. I almost laughed to see her so amazed.

"Exquisite singing," whispered Quentin.

"She must have Trolavian blood," said Belle.

The rats had been transfixed, but their reverie did not last. Before long, one of them belched. Another laughed. And within a few seconds, they were themselves again.

"The dog! The dog! The three-legged dog!"

"Silence."

And they obeyed.

"Charming," said the Piper. "Very charming indeed, little songbird. And as for you, my young blind friend, I think you'll do. Yes. I think you'll do very nicely."

And that, Penelope, was when the Piper spoke the words that I must choke back now when I read the insults on the lips of Mellon and his gang. The Piper spoke the words, and as the rabble roared their approval, Ulysses jumped back on his three legs and bayed in fright. Sophy and Quentin both fainted dead away.

"Impossible!" cried Belle.

"Mercy save us, Goose," said Scally.

The Piper came down from his throne and, while the cheering throng looked on, scooped up the rat that had once been Alloway, put him in his pocket, and stalked from the room.

40

speaking the spell

The sentry slammed the door on the cage and turned the lock.

"Yep. You were funny, all right! That was some show. Now you can keep the little songbird company while we get your rooms ready. I'm sure you'll like the accommodations we have in mind. Deluxe!"

And he stalked from the hall laughing, the key jingling on his belt.

"Just you wait, my friend," muttered Scally. "I'll show you a thing or two before we're done."

Belle did her best to revive the languishing Quentin, and I knelt beside my sister.

"Sophy."

She stirred.

"Sophy, wake up."

Ulysses whined. He licked Sophy's face. She opened her eyes. She shrank back. And little wonder. She had never before had the privilege of meeting either dragon or Trolavian.

"Stay away! Leave me alone!"

"Sophy! It's me. Penelope!"

She looked at me, disbelieving. Her face hardened.

"No. No. This is another of his tricks."

"It's no trick," said Scally. "You don't take me for just any old calico cat, do you?"

"Sophy!" I said, almost laughing. "Your eyes! Like two big moons!"

By now she was on her feet and pressing her back against the bars of the cage.

"But you can't be my sister. And you," she said to Scally, "you can't be—no. No. It's just not possible."

"All true," sang Belle, and Sophy's eyes widened further at the sound of her lovely voice.

Quentin was sitting up by now.

"Quentin," I said, "have you got your sewing kit?"

He reached into his pouch and found it.

"Would you mind?" I asked.

He took his scissors. He snipped his flawless seam. The hide parted at the forehead.

"Oh," said Sophy when she saw my grin beaming from the face of Machalus.

"Oh," she said, and went several shades of white.

"I find it helps," said Quentin, "if you put your head between your knees."

"But how?" she asked, looking from one to the next to the next. "How have you—"

And as best we could, we told her.

"Little sister," she said finally, wrapping me in her arms, "did I not tell you that your elevening would be a day you would always remember?"

"Sophy, where are the others?"

"Others?"

"The children. Ludwan. Waldef. Clemence. Ogilvie. All the rest."

"But you have seen them, Penelope."

"Seen them? Where?"

"In the hall, of course."

I was slow to understand.

"But there were no children. There were only rats."

"Yes, Penelope. That is just what I mean. You saw only rats. Some were born rats. Others were not."

Her meaning settled.

"The children?"

She nodded.

"All of them? As he did with Alloway?"

"All except for me," she answered ruefully. "He keeps me as I am so that I can sing for him. His little songbird, as you heard."

"But they were awful, Sophy. The children of Hamelin would never have been so rude!"

"It is part of the transformation, Penelope. I saw it happen. He made me watch. For the first little while, they were like themselves. But within a few hours they had become—"

"Ratty," said Scally, with great disdain.

"Terrible," said Belle.

"What do you suppose he meant," asked Quentin, "when he said to Alloway, 'You'll do?' "

"I don't know, exactly," answered Sophy. "I only know that he has something in mind. Some plan he has been laying.

Something dangerous."

Dangerous. I remembered the word on Ebba's lips. Dangerous. And suddenly I knew what the Piper was about. I could see it, like a hazy magic lantern slide projected onto a wall.

Somewhere, a harp that had been playing a long, long time was giving itself over to silence. Somewhere, an old spell was weakening. Somewhere, in a deep and tangled forest, in a house covered with vines, Cuthbert's flesh-and-blood brother was beginning to stir. And on this island fortress, in the middle of a sea made of dreaming, the Piper was assembling the troops he needed to be there for his own waking. The blind harper Alloway could somehow be of service. But how? I would have to find out.

"Having a chat, are we?"

It was the sentry. I ducked back into my dragon skin just in time.

"Sorry to break up your tea party, but the master wants the songbird. I think you're going on a little trip. Lucky, lucky, lucky."

He opened the cage. She held back.

"Come on, come on. Haven't got all day. Get a move on!"

There was nothing for it. Sophy left the cage. The sentry shoved her on. She turned to wave. And then she was gone.

"What will become of her?" asked Scally.

"What will become of us?" asked Quentin.

"If I were really Elite Guard material," said Belle, "I could surely think of something."

I said nothing. I was gathering nerve. It was time for me to travel, too, this time on my own.

"Quentin."

"Yes, Penelope?"

"Get me out of this skin."

"No, Goose," said Scally. "It's too risky. If the Piper sees you—"

"He won't," I said. "He won't see me."

"I can't allow this," said Belle. "The Magistrate—"

"The Magistrate is not here, Belle. Quentin. Please."

Out came the scissors, and the seams were rent.

"Prop Machalus up so he looks as if he's sleeping. That way the guards won't know I'm missing if they happen by."

I turned my mind inward. I shut out everything but the certainty that I must do what I was about to do. I called to mind the Piper's words, the words he had spoken to Alloway. I turned them back on myself. I heard my brave companions gasp.

"Goose!" cried Scally, horrified at what he saw.

And without looking back, I scampered through the bars of the cage and into the fortress, in search of all the other rats.

41

what Rats Know

Harpy, Harpy, Scarface, that's the name for you.
Nasty as a badger, vicious as a shrew.

That is the most recent offering from Mellon and his boys, Penelope. I know that they are more to be pitied than scorned.

I know that they are children and that they say thoughtless things. I know that they might one day regret their insolence and wish they could apologize. I know all this, and still I loathe them. Is that too strong a word? No. I do loathe them. I think they are beyond rehabilitation. If I could bring them face to face with a real harpy, I would gladly do so. A real harpy would make short work of them.

The best I could do with the spell or two I know would be nothing compared to what a harpy would serve up. Nonetheless, it would be satisfying for me to see the felon called Mellon relocated to the body of a rat. For I know what the world looks like when you scuttle along with a rat's eye view. I know how a tail feels when it drags along the ground, how smells that cause humans to recoil make a rat's mouth water. I know something about rat logic, rat hopes, rat fears. There is much I could tell you, Penelope, had I the time, about what it is like to lead a rat's life.

From the very moment my two legs became four and my nose went pink, my mind was full of ratty thoughts. I understood well enough how the children of Hamelin had become the vile, profane creatures we had seen. I also understood that I could not let rattiness take over, or I would never be able to reclaim myself. How long did I have before my nature would change, as it had with my friends? I could not worry about that. First, I had to find them.

I know now that you can never really appreciate the word "scurry" unless you have been a rat. As I scurried through the fortress I repeated to myself, "I am Penelope, daughter of Govan, daughter of Ebba, sister of Sophy. I am eleven. And here are the words that will make me again who I really am." And then I rehearsed the words of the charm that had changed me; the words that, I had to believe, would also change me back again. But if I forgot the charm, all would be lost.

Where to go, though? Where to go? I ran up one dim corridor and down another, from one hallway to the next, sniffing, always sniffing for the scent of rat. Which was now my own scent too. "I am Penelope, daughter of Govan, daughter of Ebba, sister of Sophy. I am eleven. And here are the words that will make me again who I really am."

A sound. I stopped. I listened. Again. What? Oh! Oh, my. That. That melody. That music. The Piper. His tune.

"I am Penelope."

I remembered the dream I had had on the last night of my hearing. The tune I'd heard the Piper play. This was it. The same melody. High and sweet. Seductive.

"Daughter of Govan, daughter of Ebba."

The music drew me to it. Sucked me up like a whirlpool. A wind funnel.

"Sister of Sophy."

The flagstone floor was rough on my tiny pink feet. My small heart was pounding. Find them! Find them!

"I am eleven."

Round one corner, down one hall, through one door and then another, down some stairs, down another corridor, up more stairs, up and up, through a passageway, into a tower. And there. There they were.

"And here are the words—"

A current of brown. A torrent of tails. Following the Piper

through a door in the tower wall. A door that had no reason to be there. A door that led to nothing but the open air, and a great drop onto the rocky beach below.

"And here are the words—"

The rats passed through and were changed into shimmer. They were absorbed by the air. And I knew what this was. This was the border. They were leaving the country. Passing from Deep Dreaming into the world of waking. Join them!

"Here are the words—"

Join them!

"The words—"

Join!

"Words—"

Dear Penelope. I had never felt before, nor have I felt since, so overwhelming an urge. That music filled me with longing. It was the sweetest invitation. Dance with me. Stay with me forever. Be mine. Just give in. Life as a rat. Would it be so bad?

"I am—"

What was my name?

"Penelope! Daughter of Govan! Daughter of Ebba! Sister of—"

Did I have a sister?

"Sophy! Sophy! And here are the words—"

No. They were gone. I did not want them. My feet took over. It was as though I had a great wind at my back, pushing me towards my brother rats, my sister rats, my family of rats. My destiny. At last.

"The words—"

And now I was among them. Their fur against my fur. Their whiskers on my whiskers. Belonging. This was what I had always wanted. Ahead of me there was nothing but music and shimmer. I would leave this dream. I would enter the world of waking, happy in my new life.

"Words—"

No!

"—that will make me—"

I was a war of wills, with everything that was ratty battling against everything I had been.

"Here are the words."

The words surfaced, like a drowning swimmer coming up for one last gulp of air, foul on my ratty tongue. I spat them out. They fell over my whiskers, my ratty lips. And in the snap of a finger I stood again on two legs, shaking, with the last of the rats winding between my ankles, running over my sandals, brushing against my human flesh, turning into shimmer, passing out of dream. The last was through. And then the music was gone. In its place was deep silence. And then, a croaking, hungry laugh.

42

The Harpy

A croaking, hungry laugh. An appalling smell. An unearthly stink. The ungodly waft of death. Terrible for us, but a heady perfume for carrion creatures. Vultures. Buzzards. Rats. Harpies.

"What have we here? My, my, my."

I looked up into the wide, vaulted dome that was the ceiling of the room. Face of a hag. Body of a bird. Long, sharp claws. She squinted down from her perch upon a high beam.

"A funny girly interloper. My, my, my."

Every word was carried on a wind that came from the deep and filthy reaches of her body.

"Quite the stunt, little one. Quite the stunt. Ratty rat one instant, girly girl the next. My, my, my."

That breath.

"In all my years as border guard, I've never seen anything like it. How did you do it? No. Don't bother answering. I'm sure it's a fascinating story, but I suspect it might be on the long side, and I'm starved. Famished. So hard to scrape together a decent meal around here. The odd crumb. The odd bit of cheese. The occasional rat that sickens and dies and gets thrown my way. But truly, it's been an eternity since I had the flesh of a girly girl. My, my, my."

A rasping chuckle on a gale of malodorous air.

"I imagine that you wanted to cross the border, but as you can see, it's closed. I think it may be closed for good. Of course, no one tells me anything, but I hear rumors, and I gather the Piper has no intention of coming back. And what does that mean for me? For poor old harpy? I guess that means I'm out of a job, doesn't it? And here I was feeling sorry for myself. Just a little bitter that there was no gold watch, no retirement party, no bonus check, no rousing chorus of 'For she's a jolly good fellow.' Down in the dumps, I was! Then, poof! You come along. My, my, my."

She spread her feathers, and a rain of rancid crumbs fell down. She flapped her wings slowly. She rose from her perch. She made a leisurely ascent to the top of the dome and did a turn or two around it, grinning down at me all the while.

"My, my, my. Don't move, girly. I'm coming down for a closer look."

One by one she unsheathed her talons. She angled them in my direction. She folded her wings. But before she could drop down to finish me off, the air was rent by a warlike cry. A single note, shrill and thrilling.

"Yeeeeaaaaiiiiieeee!"

It stopped the harpy cold.

"What in the world?"

"Yeeeeaaaaiiiiieeee!"

The sound split the air. The harpy looked over her shoulder. Following her glance, I saw the source of the bellicose blast.

"Belle!"

"Hellfire and damnation!" hissed the harpy. "Just when things were looking up."

"Yeeeeaaaaiiiiieee! Leave her alone, you filth-mongering monster!"

"Belle! But how did you—"

"Stand away, Penelope!" she sang.

Belle was a blur of fury and purpose. She whirled into the room, spitting sparks of anger like a Catherine wheel. She sighted her foe and flew straight for her. She ducked under the harpy's awful belly, landed a thudding punch, then swooped up above her and struck her a loud blow squarely on the head.

"Take that, you great putrid menace!"

The harpy released a terrible volley of stinking curses.

"Watch your tongue, you repulsive great corpse eater! There are ladies in the room."

And again Belle landed a blow to the harpy's chest that sent her reeling back against the wall.

"Yippayippayappaodalaydeeoooooo!" Belle yodeled triumphantly as the harpy began to tumble. She didn't let up. She was on the harpy in a flash, beating her with her wings, kicking her with her long, strong rabbitlike legs. I watched in awe, for Belle had never shown herself to me as anything but the gentlest of beings.

"Trolavians forever!" she caroled, and redoubled her pummeling with both feet and wings.

But while the harpy had been badly battered, she was far from done for. She disgorged a stream of carbolic spittle that caught Belle squarely in the eye. Belle howled, as much from disgust as from pain, and for the briefest of seconds she let down her guard. It was all the time the harpy needed. She flipped herself onto her back and locked her jaws around Belle's ankles. Belle howled. She struck back with her strong, leathery wings, raining down a series of blows that scattered harpy feathers left and right. But the harpy would not release her grip. She brought her own feet into the fray and began raking at Belle's wings with her long, sharp claws. Belle twisted and turned, desperate to free herself. The harpy gathered strength. She struck a second time, a third and a fourth. Every blow was accompanied by the sound of tearing, and by Belle's cries, each one more pained than the last.

My heart sank as I watched the tide turn in their airborne battle. I was powerless to help Belle, could do nothing but watch her tumble. The harpy was right on top of her, biting and tearing wherever she could. Finally, she took hold of Belle by the neck, shook her vigorously, and flung her to the floor.

"Belle!"

"Penelope," she sang. "I am so sorry—"

"No, Belle! Don't move. I'll—"

But the harpy was right beside us.

"My lucky day! An entree and a dessert. I think I'll finish off the soldier girl first!"

She reared and snarled.

"No!" I screamed. I tried to throw myself between the harpy and my fallen friend. I felt the graze of claw, then the warm rush of blood.

"Penelope!" gasped Belle, trying to pull herself to her feet.

"Girly blood! That smells good! My, my, my! I can't wait to—"

Those were the harpy's last words. The last sound she heard was a long, deep howl. The last thing she saw was a streak of black. Then she lay dead at my feet, her throat in the mouth of three-legged Ulysses.

Everything was slow and hazy, as though the air had thickened. As though the room were wrapped in gauze. I knelt over Belle, scarcely aware that Quentin and Scally had come panting to my side.

"Oh, Penelope. I have let you down. I have failed."

"No, Belle. No. You were so brave!"

"The Magistrate—"

"The Magistrate would have been proud. He *will* be proud. He'll make you a Colonel. Fergus and Bergus will be so envious. You'll get a medal. There'll be a parade."

"No, Penelope. No medals. No parade. I am done. I am dying."

"Belle! Don't be silly."

But there was the green stickiness pooling around my knees. Trolavian blood.

"Your face . . ."

"It's nothing, Belle."

"Lean down."

I bent close. I looked into her sad, dimming Trolavian eyes.

"Closer."

I did. With the last bit of strength left to her, she raised her head and kissed the gash on my cheek. A current of heat passed through it and tattered skin met tattered skin. The wound closed over. The bleeding stopped.

"A little Trolavian trick. Good-bye, Penelope."

All the many atoms that made her began to vibrate, began to hum. We watched in sad amazement as she turned from flesh into pulse into light. For a second or two the whole room glowed with everything that had once been Belle. And then she was gone. All that was left of her was a song, high and sad and wordless, hanging in the air. We stood in silence. We listened until her song was gone. Until we could hear no more.

43

mourning

Deep Dreaming is a rare gift, Penelope. A gift that marked me in more ways than one. Was I lucky to receive it? I can't say. If all the gifts in the world were lined up before me now, would I choose Deep Dreaming? I wonder. In truth, it has little to recommend it. Unlike the gift of singing, say, or of dancing, it is difficult to share with others. Deep Dreaming is not easily explained or understood, not even by those who practice it. Unlike a gift for carpentry or gardening, it leaves you with nothing to show for all your trouble. What's more, it does not endure.

Deep Dreaming belongs to the young, for it requires strength of mind and heart. Concentration. It makes intense demands on the body. It can be undertaken by one who lacks vitality, but only at very great risk. There is always the danger that the system will fail, you see. That the heart will stop laboring, the body cave in. When that happens, a severing occurs. The Deep Dreamer is cut loose. She becomes homeless. A ghost.

This was why Cuthbert knew that he could not travel in search of the children of Hamelin. And it was why his brother had become so dangerous. Locked away, hidden so well that not even Time could find him, as Cuthbert had said, the Piper was spared the indignities of age. His young body sustained the Dreamer, and the Dreamer grew in power and in anger. His would be a terrible waking.

In the end, luck and choice make no difference. Deep Dreaming is what I was given, for better or for worse. It made me who I am. And whether I wanted it or not, it showed me that there is more to the world than meets the eye. More wonder. More evil. More courage. More sorrow.

Sorrow. I did not even know what it was before Belle died. When her final song faded, there was no sign that she had ever been among us. The only proof was the ache in our hearts and the hideous evidence of the fallen harpy.

Ulysses lay by his vanquished prey, panting. Quentin stood in the place where Belle had been and choked out her name over and over.

"I never thought I could grow so fond of a Trolavian," he gulped. "All those stories I heard about how they were monsters . . ."

Scally threaded himself around my ankles. I picked him up. I held him close. There is nothing quite so comforting, to my way of thinking, as a warm cat pressed against the heart.

"I am pleased to find you safe and looking more or less yourself, Goose. When last I saw you, you were sporting whiskers and a tail."

"I'm glad to see you too, Scally. How did you escape the cage?"

"We can thank Quentin for that," answered Scally. "You would have been proud of him, Goose."

"It was Belle's idea," snuffled Quentin. "I would never have thought of it myself."

"What happened?"

"After you left, she went quite mad with worry. She was

pulling at the bars of the cage, trying to bend them apart so that she could chase after you. But they wouldn't budge, not even a fraction. And then finally—"

Here again he burst into a tempest of tears. Scally picked up the story.

"Belle said to him, 'Quentin. If you can use your dragon brain to move branches, is there any reason why you can't move iron bars?' "

"I told her I didn't think it was possible," continued Quentin, doing his best to control his sobbing. "I told her that no dragon had ever worked with anything but wood. We specialize in vegetable, not mineral. And she said—"

His shoulders were heaving, and again he looked to Scally for assistance.

"She said, 'Then you must be the first, Quentin. So much depends on it!' "

"I said that I couldn't, that I didn't know how, but she insisted and insisted until finally I just stood back and—and—well, I don't quite know what I did."

"Whatever it was, it worked," Scally said. "The bars began to tremble and hum. Finally they spread as easily as warm butter. Belle let out a whoop and she was gone, with Ulysses tearing after her. It is a pity he's a dog. He would make an excellent cat."

"We hurried as fast as we could, but by the time we got here—"

And then Quentin's sobs came fast and furious. Ulysses raised his head and bayed out his loud grief. I am 101 years old, Penelope. I have seen much death, as will anyone who lives this long. I am no stranger to mourning. But I think I can say I have never felt so heartsick as I did then, in that room, standing on the spot where my courageous friend had died. I had not known Belle long, but I had come to love her. Her melodic voice. Her modesty. Her easy strength and quiet fortitude. We could never have come so far without her. And now, how would we go on? I held Scally tighter, as if by squeezing him I could wring out an answer.

"When we get home, Goose, you must have a bath right away. You smell rather strongly of rat," he said. He put a paw to my cheek. "You will have a scar. A souvenir to remember her by." He nodded in the direction of the harpy. She did not smell any sweeter in death than she had in life.

I touched it, this long welt, traced its path from my ear to my chin. Suddenly, I wanted to see it.

"Quentin, do you still have your compact?"

He nodded.

"May I borrow it?"

He reached into his pouch and handed me the small gold case. I opened it and gazed into the mirror. Chaotic hair. Eyes red-rimmed from crying. My too-long nose and too-thin mouth. And my new scar, thick and fierce. Purple and engorged.

"Goose," said Scally gently, "enough."

I couldn't stop staring. Tears came. The mirror blurred. I blinked them back. Still the glass was misted and gray. I blinked once more, and the image came into focus.

"Cuthbert!"

"My brave Penelope."

"Oh, Cuthbert! So much has happened. Belle has died, and the Piper has disappeared, and Alloway was turned into a rat, and so were all the children, and Sophy is—"

"You must listen, Penelope. I cannot speak long. My powers are waning, and time is running out. You have come too far and endured much too much to lose heart now. You must muster all your strength and confidence. You must believe in yourself. No one could do what you have done without a profound gift of Deep Dreaming. Now, you must put it to the greatest test. Now, you must move into the world of the waking."

"But I don't know how. I don't know—"

"You do know, just as you know how to breathe, Penelope."

"But what about Quentin? He belongs to the dreaming world. How can I leave him behind?"

"If you allow Quentin to come, he can. You can hold open the curtain for him. But you must hurry."

"Hurry where?"

"Goose! Look! The door!"

I glanced from the mirror and saw that the door through which the Piper had passed had shed its solidity. What had been wood was now shimmer.

"Hurry," said Cuthbert. His image faded, and my own face reemerged from the mirror.

It was Ulysses who took the lead. He heaved himself up onto his three legs, barked twice, and leaped through what seconds before had been thick planks and heavy hinges.

"Come on!" I called. "We all have to go. Quentin. You next."

He began to tremble. For one dreadful moment, I thought he was going to faint.

"Go!" I yelled, but he stood stock-still, staring.

"Oh, for goodness' sake," said Scally. He jumped up onto the dragon's shoulders and dug in his claws.

"Ouch!"

"Go!" commanded Scally. "Now! Giddyup!"

With my cat still clinging fast to his back, the dragon took a flying leap. I was right behind them, diving head first, out of the world of dreaming.

Section vi

The waking

44

Into the Forest

I saw Mellon last week in the market. He was with his mother and father. They looked pleasant enough. The sort of folk who would help out a neighbor, or with whom you could exchange some village news. Ordinary folk. Quiet folk. They were preoccupied with the price of potatoes and had their backs turned when Mellon stuck out his tongue and made a rude gesture in my direction.

Where does it come from, then, Mellon's cruelty? I see none of it in his parents. Did he learn it somewhere else? Or was he made that way? If he is already rotten at the core, wouldn't the world be better off without him? Why shouldn't he spend the rest of his time on earth as a rat?

I have no more chance of penetrating Mellon's ways than I do of understanding why the kernel of evil took root in the Piper. The Piper. In a way, it is a pity that he and I never had a chance to compare notes about Deep Dreaming. After all, there were not many like us. Not many who could divide in two, one half in trance and the other half wandering. The Piper and I could have had fascinating conversations, I feel quite sure. But it was not to be. By the time we finally met, he was not in the mood for a prolonged chinwag. Nor, come to that, was I.

I followed my companions through the shimmering door and into the world of waking. As I had twice before, I found myself tumbling. Beneath me was not the windswept sea that surrounded the Piper's fortress. Rather, I hurtled earthward towards a forest, green and tall and vast. From my great height, I could see how its outline formed a pattern. An elegant curve of neck. A gentle swoop of breast. This forest looked exactly like a harp.

"The trees that Cuthbert charmed," I thought, and then I was on the ground and rolling, over and over, down a steep, grassy hill. By the time I fetched up at the bottom I was giddy and breathless. I lay still, staring into the sky from which I'd come, watching the clouds whirl and then slow. I tested my limbs, one after the other. I was relieved to detect the far-off song of a plaintive thrush. For the time being at least, I still had my hearing. A face appeared in my frame of vision. Then a second. Then a third. My companions.

"A remarkable entrance, Goose," said Scally. "Better even than your somersault skip."

"Are you in one piece?" asked Quentin, peering anxiously into my eyes. Ulysses gave my face a thorough licking.

"That the dog is brave I can't deny, but why must he slobber so?" asked Scally, disdainfully. "Why that kind can't manage their tongues with more finesse is a mystery I'll never fathom." And as if by way of demonstration, he gave his own paw a delicate lick.

"Where are we?" asked Quentin, more concerned with practicality.

I dislodged the cat from my chest. I sat up and surveyed the terrain. We were at a forest edge. The same forest, I supposed, that I had seen while tumbling.

"We're where we're meant to be," I answered. "At least, I hope so."

"Do you hear something?" asked Scally.

I listened.

"I hear it too," said Quentin.

And so did I. Far in the distance rang a tune that was both familiar and unsettling. It was the melody I had heard in the piper's fortress and in the dream on my elevening eve. But this time, the music was not played on a flute. This music was made by a harp. And no ordinary harp, either. I knew it right away, knew it in the way a mother knows the cry of her own baby. Eight strings. A driftwood frame. It was the harp I had made for Alloway. That his fingers plucked the strings I had no doubt.

Nor did Ulysses. He began to bay and run frantically in search of a pathway into the forest, but there was none.

"I've never seen so thick a stand of trees," said Scally. "Like a solid wall."

"We won't get through," said Quentin.

"We have to. Quentin. Listen. Remember how you freed Belle when she was caught in the branches? And how you bent the bars in the cage?"

"Yes, of course."

"Then you must do the same thing now."

"With an entire forest?"

He looked dubiously at the imposing wall of trees.

"It's our only chance, Quentin."

He took a step backward. He wore the look of someone who was thinking very, very hard. He fixed his gaze firmly on the impenetrable forest. We watched and waited, scarcely drawing a breath. Nothing happened. Nothing budged.

"It's no good. I can't do it."

"You must, Quentin. For us. And for Belle, too."

He turned away to dab a sudden tear. He sniffed. Then he shook his head to banish the sadness and straightened his spine. He stood resolute and strong. "For Belle," he repeated.

Once again Quentin faced the forest. Once again he assumed an expression of deep concentration. Within a few seconds, the trunks closest to us began to shiver and bend, first one, then another, then tree after tree in ever more rapid succession. Opposing trunks curved from root to crown so that they resembled a long row of archery bows. Where once the trees had been a solid wall, now they presented a long and leafy tunnel.

"You did it, Quentin. You did it!" I cheered.

"Brilliant work," agreed Scally.

But there was no more time for praise or congratulations. Our path was clear. With the panting Ulysses leading us on, we made our way swiftly into the dark and beating heart of the forest.

45

A Lucky Horseshoe

Shortly, Penelope, you will come here with your father. Then the harp called Alloway will pass into your keeping, as will these many pages. I wonder what you will make of them. Will they amuse you, or will you think they are the ramblings of a mad old woman? Will you keep them to yourself? Or will you share them with others? The choice is yours, of course, but I rather hope that one day you will decide to make them public. Perhaps I flatter myself, but I think that mine is a story worth the telling. Anyone would want to hear it, I should think, on a cold winter's night by a crackling fire. Little children would interrupt impatiently.

"Did they make it through the woods?"

"Did they find the Piper?"

"Did they come back home again?"

Good questions, all of them. And I will have just time enough to set down the answers before you and Micah pay me your final visit.

We entered the somber woods, leaving the light behind. Ulysses was not young, and he ran on only three legs, but even so we could not match his pace. He galloped with purposeful ease over the roots and moss that carpeted the forest floor. Scally and Quentin and I were winded by the time we caught up with him, at the edge of a clearing. Panting, we hid ourselves behind the thick-waisted trees to look out upon a most shocking scene.

Vicious rats stood guard over a tangle of twisted tendrils and vines heaped in the middle of the glen like an enormous ball of twine. The Piper, dressed as always in his green and yellow garments, strode up and down on his long, thin legs, now and then pausing to spit out an order.

"Faster!"

"Harder!"

And there before us we saw the children of Hamelin. Nan and Elfleda. Bridget and Newlyn. Petra, Osmanna, and

Ninnoc and Rayne. Some of them had axes and some of them had hoes. Some had only sharp-edged rocks. As if in a trance, they cut and sawed at the thick sinews of vegetation.

"Be quick, you little fools! Hurry! Hurry!"

Ulfrid and Richard. Kea and Radegun. Brigid and Maura and Cannice and Joan. All the children of Hamelin were here. Their bodies and faces had been restored, but they were no more themselves than when I had seen them as rioting rats.

"Look at Sophy," said Quentin. "And oh, poor Alloway."

They stood apart from the others. My heart broke at the sight of them. Alloway held the little harp I'd made and plucked from its strings the Piper's hypnotic spell. He might have been a clockwork toy, his playing was so mechanical. Sophy hummed the same melody, swaying gently from side to side.

"What are they doing?" whispered Quentin.

"Freeing the Piper," answered Scally, and I knew he was right. Under the tangle of vines was a long-locked house. In the house, a slowing harp. Beside the harp, a sleeping man. Sleeping now—but not for long.

"Well, Goose. What shall we do?"

It was a simple question with a simple answer: Stop the Piper and free the children. But it did not come with a simple plan in tow.

"I don't know. We have to get into the house, that much is sure."

"But how, Goose?"

I was asking myself the same thing.

A short distance away, Ulysses was working with frantic determination, kicking up a cloud of earth and leaf mold, digging as best he could with his one front leg. He whimpered as he pawed at the earth.

"Distracted by a bone at a time like this," said Scally, disgustedly. "How like a dog."

"Hush, Ulysses," I whispered. I went to see what he was up to, worried that his whining would attract the attention of the guards.

Ulysses wagged his tail and ran in a circle around his excavation. He stopped every few seconds to pull with his mouth at something on the ground.

"What have you found?" I asked, as I reached to take it from his jaws. It appeared to be a horseshoe, but it was attached to something I couldn't see.

"Scally. Quentin. Come here."

I fell onto my hands and knees and cleared away the rest of the debris. There lay a door, such as might be seen on a root cellar. What I had taken for a horseshoe was its handle. I grabbed hold and hauled up, but the door didn't budge.

"Let me help," said Quentin, taking hold beside me. "On the count of three, Penelope. One. Two."

And on three we gave a mighty tug. We felt the door give slightly.

"One. Two. Three."

This time the door grudgingly creaked open, disturbing a colony of long-legged centipedes that scuttled for cover. To our great astonishment, we found that we were staring down into a tunnel. Its long-sealed mouth exhaled unpleasant mustiness, but an exciting sound rose from its throat. A single note, long and sonorous.

"Goose. A harp?"

"I think so."

Another note came from the earth, and then I was certain. A harp, yes, and certainly not Alloway's. A very slow harp. A harp whose dying song echoed down a subterranean corridor. I had found my way in.

Scally leapt into action. "Let's hurry, Goose," he said, preparing to enter the tunnel.

"On the double," agreed Quentin.

I shook my head. Hearing the slowing harp had given me an idea.

"No," I said, firmly. "I'll go alone."

"But Goose—"

"No, Scally. Now listen."

Very briefly, I outlined my strategy.

"I'm with you, Goose."

"Quentin?"

"Yes."

"Quick! Hurry! Harder!"

The Piper's voice grew ever more sharp and eager as he paced up and down. We waited until he had stalked out of view.

"Now, Quentin!"

"Wish me luck," he said, as he reached into his pouch and pulled out his skipping rope.

"Good luck, my friend."

"And to you."

Taking his rope in paw, he entered the clearing and gaily capered about.

Jump! I am a dragon.
Jump! That's plain to see.
Jump! I am a dragon
And you can't catch me!

The children stared blankly into the air as they continued to hack at the vines. The guard rats, however, gaped in amazement.

Jump! My name is Quentin.
Jump! I'm hard to fault.
Jump! And now I'll try to skip
A daring somersault.

A somersault skip. He was bound and determined. While every rat stared, open-mouthed, the dreamtime dragon heaved himself into the air of the waking world. And it was then that our attack began. Scally and Ulysses moved in from separate flanks, laying waste to the ranks of rats with considerable glee. I almost longed for the deafness I knew was waiting for me, for terrible gnashing and howling filled the air. Whisker and tail flew left and right as I turned my back on the carnage and made my way into the tunnel.

46

The Piper's Room

It has just gone midnight. My old clock has pealed its twelve deep gongs. I do not hear them, Penelope, but I feel them.

Their wide vibrations pass over me, like waves wash over a swimmer. They pass through me, like light shines through a prism. And their singing reminds me that I must give your harp, your Alloway, one last tuning before you come for it. I will pluck each string. I will make each string hum. I will know by the way each note feels against my fingers, my knees, my thighs, if it is pitched too low or too high.

It is very satisfactory, my method, and I am not sure which I resent more: the scorn of Mellon and his henchmen for my deafness, or the pity of those who think I am somehow diminished because I don't hear with my ears. Those who feel this way are wrong, for I have learned to hear music with my whole body. And it was in the Piper's house that I had my first lesson in how this could be so.

Into the dark and airless tunnel I went. I can only suppose that the tunnel was meant to be used but this once, for earth rained down behind me as I hurried forward. The way ahead remained clear, but the path behind was blocked forever.

The roof of the tunnel was just high enough to accommodate my head, and I ran without stooping, tracing the walls with my fingertips until the passage came to an abrupt end. Blind as a mole in sunlight, I ran my hands along the cold, flat wall while pebbles and clods hailed down around me. At last I felt a latch and handle. The door swung wide. As I fell across the threshold into the Piper's house, another harp note swam through the air and enveloped me. It was an ominous welcome. This room, its windows covered in vines, was only marginally brighter than the tunnel had been. Breathless, I turned back to the door from which I had just emerged. But my groping revealed no latch. No seam. No sign that anything like a door had ever been there.

Slowly, my eyes struck a bargain with the gloom. I was in a round entryway with stairways to the left and right. A long corridor lay before me. Which way to go?

Another note. A trembling. A caress. A long and slow vibration that touched my heart before it reached my ear. I listened for the music again. Listened with my whole body, this time. And there it was. Rich and slow and distant. I hurried through rooms and halls, past bolted doors, up a stairway. Listen. Go left. A door. Listen. Oh. Open. Oh. Oh.

The room was sparsely furnished. A chest of drawers, upon which lay a few thick and dusty books. A tall wardrobe with a long mirror. Two narrow cots, side by side, each beneath an elaborate canopy of cobwebs. One cot was empty and unmade, the bedclothes in a heap. And on the other lay the sleeping Piper. His arms were folded across his chest, and in one hand he clutched a flute, a simple reed. This must have been the first of his magic pipes, fashioned so many years ago while he still lived only in the world of waking. It was unnerving to see him when I knew he was also outside, urging on his slaves. I had a sudden image of *my* other self, lying on her bed in Hamelin. I wondered if we would ever be reunited.

The warm, slow pulse of another note drew me back. There it was. Next to the Piper's bed. The harp was also draped in a shroud of cobwebs. I brushed them aside. The instrument was beautiful. Expertly carved. And that sound! Rich and embracing. But slow. So slow. Soon the space between the notes would stretch on forever. The weakening spell would die. And what would happen then was what I had to prevent. But how?

"Oh, Cuthbert," I said aloud, looking down at my friend's sleeping brother. "What am I to do?"

But it was not his voice that answered.

" 'Cuthbert.' Why am I not surprised to hear you speak that name?"

And I turned from the Piper to look at the Piper. His cold, thin smile. His wide, angry eyes. I had not heard his footfalls, but now he was with me in the room. I had never felt so alone.

47

The piper wakes

Feeling alone is not always a bad thing. Solitude becomes a habit, Penelope. For me, by now, it is a habit of very long standing. I am not much accustomed to receiving even occasional visitors, let alone one that wants to move in. But that is what the Shadow seems to have in mind, the Shadow that has been my companion these last several days. What a nuisance he is! He snoops. He finds things. A letter opener. A bread knife. A dusty green bottle. And he talks to me as well.

"Look, Penelope. Look what I have here."

"A skipping rope! Where was it?"

"In the attic. May I?"

He gave the rope a twirl.

"I'd like to see you try!"

The Shadow was awkward at first, but he caught on soon enough. I have to admit that he is agile. And tireless, it seems. He has been skipping for a solid hour now.

Come with me, Penelope.
Take me by the hand!
I would like to show you
How we live in Shadowland!

"Quiet, Shadow."

"Come skip."

"You know I'm too old for such nonsense. And even if I could, I wouldn't."

"Why not?"

"I have work to do, Shadow. I haven't much time."

That set him pouting. Not that I care. I can hardly worry about some shadow's feelings. Not when my story is so nearly done. Not when I am remembering that dangerous day when I was small, fearful, and not long eleven, looking into the Piper's malevolent eyes.

"Is it you I can thank for the carnival outside?"

I didn't answer. He grabbed my shoulders and glared at me, unblinking.

"Your name?"

"Penelope."

"Ah. The little songbird's sister, no?"

I said nothing.

"So different. She is lovely. But you—"

He touched my scarred cheek with a long finger.

"I recognize my harpy's calling card."

I tried to turn away, but the Piper held my chin. He leaned in close. He spoke my name slowly, weighing its every syllable on his tongue.

"Pen-el-o-pe. So this is who Cuthbert sends as his Deep Dreaming emissary. Cuthbert the good. Cuthbert the brave. Cuthbert, my traitorous brother."

A harp note, as soft and as low as a sigh. The Piper waited until it had died away before speaking again. His voice was quiet, but there was no mistaking the anger that coursed beneath the surface.

"What did Cuthbert intend? That you would somehow set the harp to playing again?"

Another note, so feeble it could hardly penetrate the air.

"He never—"

"Because that will not happen."

He twisted my head in the direction of the harp.

"Look."

I saw its thickest string waver. I felt, more than heard, the vibrations of a deep, faint note. Then the instrument shuddered and slipped into silence. One by one, its strings snapped in two.

"Over and done!" cried the Piper, exultantly. "At long last, it is done!"

He shoved me aside and flew across the room. He pulled the cobwebs from around the cot. He picked up his sleeping self and began to dance, turning and turning in a crazy waltz. As the ragdoll limbs of his flesh-and-blood other spun out of control, the flute flew from his hand. Dry and brittle after so many years, it snapped in two when it hit the flagstone floor.

"Good riddance to it," he crowed. "I am ready for bigger things now. I am ready to wake and seize the day. No. The world!" With that, he kissed himself on the lips, and where once there had been two Pipers, now there was one. He executed a jubilant cartwheel, coming to rest before the wardrobe mirror.

"I have waited many years for this, Penelope," he said, pulling delightedly at the skin on the back of his hands. "Many, many years. How I long to make a fresh start. New clothes, for one thing. Something different from this piebald arrangement. And of course, new companions. I have grown weary of rodents and infants. And now that your friends have kindly dealt with so many of my rats, I need only dispose of the children."

"No!"

"You object," he said, with a mocking laugh. "But as I see it, I will be doing your young friends a great favor. I will save them from growing up, from becoming as deceitful and as grasping as their parents."

"You can't mean that you would kill them."

"What else would I mean? Except for my little songbird, of course. Her I plan to marry."

"No!"

"You don't approve of that either? Too bad. I had hoped that some of her family might come to the wedding. My own, alas, will be absent."

"What about Alloway?"

"The blind boy? He has exhausted his usefulness."

I wanted to ball up my fists and pummel him.

"How can you be so cruel?"

"I am simply true to my nature. What you call cruel, I call honest."

"But why choose us?"

"It was Hamelin that did the choosing. It was Hamelin that invited me in. Hamelin got what it asked for, and Hamelin got what it deserved. It might have been anywhere else, true enough. Any place governed by the greedy and the grasping would have served me just as well, but it was in your town that I found a foothold. Then, I was half asleep. Now I am eager to test my waking powers."

"But what about—"

"No, Penelope," he said, with a dismissive wave of his hand. "You are stalling. Do you hope for rescue? There is no point. The best of my rats are keeping your companions busy. When last I saw them, your friends were dodging the arrows of my archers. It is very likely that they are dead by now. The same fate awaits the children. You I will have to deal with differently, since you visit this place as a dreamer. No matter. For you there is a particular spell. I know just where to find it."

He walked to the chest of drawers, picked up the thickest of the volumes that lay upon it, and blew away the dust.

"Just a few words," he said, leafing through it, "and the link between you and your sleeping other will be severed for good. One of you will be doomed to wander eternally in a dream. The other will never wake. Never again."

Calm. I needed it now more than I ever had. I imagined my mind as a lake untroubled by waves. I willed inspiration to break through the flat surface. And suddenly, like a shiny fish, it did.

"Wait."

He looked up from his book.

"Why?"

"One more thing."

He flashed me his icy smile.

"What?"

"A favor."

"Ah," he chuckled. "The final request before execution, is that it?"

"Give me one last chance to do what I love best."

"Meaning?"

"To skip."

He threw back his head and laughed gleefully.

"Skip? How novel. Well, why not? I will give you precisely one minute to indulge your final pleasure."

I unknotted my rope from around my waist and crossed the room. I stood before the wardrobe with its long mirror. I turned once. Twice. I began to skip in earnest.

48

Three Times I Will Come

The rope hit the floor and stirred up the years of dust that had gathered there. I fought back an urge to sneeze as I watched myself in the glass. I was a sight. My wild hair bounced with each jump. My face was streaked with dirt from my passage through the tunnel. And my scar glowed a vibrant purple. But I had no time to worry about my appearance. I could think of only one person to call on for help. It had to work. It had to.

Skipping in the looking glass, skip from side to side,
Skipping in the looking glass, who will be a bride?
Who will have a wedding day, who's the one who's sought?
Who will wear the wedding dress, who will tie the knot?
Who will make the wedding ring? Who will raise the toast?
Who will bake the wedding cake? Who will be the host?
Who will give the bride away, needle, thread and pin?
Cuthbert, Cuthbert, now come in!

The book fell to the floor with a thud. The Piper was across the room in a single bound, wresting the rope from my hands. He slapped my cheeks, hard, first one, then the other. My scar burned with a searing pain.

"What kind of a game is this?"

"Cuthbert!" I called again, with a desperate glance at the mirror. Surely he had heard me. Surely he would honor his word and come a third time. But all I saw when I looked in the glass was the Piper, preparing to strike me again. I held up my hands to ward off the blow. He grabbed me by the wrists and spun me around. He held my face close to his own as he hissed out his venomous words.

"Do you think your silly skipping spell has any power here?"

He spun me around so that I faced the mirror again. He towered over me, thin and raging.

"Look. Do you see him?"

I shook my head.

"Nor will you," he said, whirling me back to face him. He shook me violently. "Cuthbert is dead."

Dead. A word so hard and raw that it made me flinch.

"He's not. He can't be!"

"But he is," the Piper sneered. "Without question. You saw the proof of it yourself when the harp stopped playing. No spell can outlive the magician who casts it. That is among the first lessons we learned as children. How disappointed our father would be to know that the golden child was not paying attention."

"Our father."

Who had spoken? It was neither my tormentor nor me who pronounced those echoing words.

"Our father."

Again. The Piper froze. He loosened his grip, and I crumpled to my knees.

"No!" he shouted.

I looked up to see him transfixed by the glass. Its surface grew hazy, then molten, before surrendering itself to a pair of kindly eyes, a lined face, a voice that was both quiet and sad.

"Our father. How dare you utter his name when you have betrayed everything he stood for?"

The Piper recoiled in shock. "Cuthbert!"

"I am glad you still know me, brother, after all this time."

"You are dead!"

"But not departed, as you can see."

"Impossible."

"Dear brother, if *you* had paid attention to our father's

lessons, you would remember that impossible was not a word we were encouraged to use."

"Go! I command you. You are not welcome here."

"Welcome or not, this is my home. Here I am and here I mean to stay."

Howling his outrage, the Piper reached the ruined harp in a single bound. The instrument was big and cumbersome, but his anger gave him the strength to lift it as if it were no heavier than a loaf of bread. He bellowed foul curses as he smashed the harp once, twice, three times into the mirror. I covered my head as the glass exploded into a thousand tiny shards. When I dared to look up again, Cuthbert stood in its place.

49

A Reunion

"Thank you for releasing me, brother. I was feeling rather confined in there."

Cuthbert walked to where I knelt on the floor. He offered his hand and helped me to my feet.

"I am glad to see you face to face again, Penelope."

"I knew you would come!"

"You have done well, my young friend. Very, very well."

The Piper kicked at the fragments of glass and let go a bitter laugh.

"Save your smug congratulations," he spat. "I am not finished yet. You can't suppose that I will allow myself to be thwarted by a ghost and a Deep Dreaming girl!"

"Perhaps not by us alone, brother. But have you forgotten our allies?"

"That ragtag company? My troops have taken care of them, I am sure."

"We think otherwise," came a familiar voice from the doorway.

"Quentin! You're safe!"

I ran to hug him.

"Oh, Quentin. You did it!"

Something soft brushed against my ankles. It was Scally, who carried in his jaws limp evidence of victory against the rodent army. He deposited the dead rat at the feet of the Piper, gave his cat whiskers a cursory wipe with his paw, and jumped into my arms.

"Just like the old days, Goose. I can't think when I've had so much fun."

The Piper looked around the room. He spoke again, and although he put on a show of bravado, I caught a flicker of something like doubt in his eyes.

"All very cozy, brother dear. What a cheerful congregation you've assembled. So powerful, too. A ghost, a girl made of dreams, a dragon of uncertain provenance, and a talking cat. An impressive inventory!"

"I would gladly take his throat," growled Scally in my ear.

"But how will your company hold up against my army of children, Cuthbert? Will your confederates be as sanguine about spilling *their* blood?"

"I pity you, brother."

"Stow your pity. I am in earnest. One measure of music,

and my slaves will storm the house, ready to attack and kill. Tell me, Penelope. Would you like to see your sister chop your pussycat in two with an axe? I need only pick up my pipe—"

But he stopped mid-phrase as he remembered the sound of his reed flute breaking in two.

"Dear brother," continued Cuthbert. "I was never as gifted as you in Deep Dreaming. Nor was music-making my talent. But you will remember that it was always I who could whistle loudest."

With that, Cuthbert put fingers to mouth and blew a shrill summons. In a blink, Ulysses appeared beside him, carrying in his mouth the driftwood harp.

The Piper looked stricken, then began to giggle.

"Do you really intend to set that absurd toy to playing?"

"It worked very well to keep the children in your thrall. I think that you too will find its melodies persuasive."

Cuthbert turned towards the doorway. "Alloway, you may come in now."

And so he came. With him was Sophy, who held him by the hand. She left his side and ran to me. She folded me in her arms, and for the first time since my dreaming had begun, I wept.

You can imagine the joyful din in that little room. And it was in the midst of that happy confusion that the Piper made his last bid for freedom. With the agility of an acrobat, he leapt high into the air. He curled himself into a tight ball and hit the ground tumbling. He rolled with incredible speed to where his book of spells had fallen.

"Stop him!" yelped Quentin, but the book was already in

the Piper's clutches. Things might have worked out very differently had it not been for the swift intervention of Ulysses.

"Damnation!" shrieked the Piper as the dog leapt towards him, flattening him on the floor. Ulysses tore the book from the Piper's grasp. Then he took hold of the piebald costume and dragged the Piper back to the center of the room as though he were a bone ripe for burying.

"Alloway," said Cuthbert, "would you be so good as to play for us?"

Alloway's fingers brushed the strings. Clear and true, the notes rose up from the little harp I'd cobbled together so hastily on that rocky strand.

"You have made a fine instrument, Penelope," said Cuthbert. "Govan would be proud. It is a pity he will not have a chance to see your work, but the harp must remain here."

"No-o-o-o-o," howled the Piper. But it was already too late. An irresistible force was drawing his eyelids down.

Alloway's playing grew in speed and confidence. I could not name the tune he coaxed from the harp, but it was oddly familiar. I opened myself up to the music. I let it pass through me. I listened as I had learned to do, as I have continued to listen since then: not with my ears, but with my whole body. That tune! Where had I heard it before? And then I knew. It was the mirror image of the song the Piper had played when he cast his net and captured the children. These were exactly the same notes, only played in reverse.

The Piper stirred. He spoke slowly, so faintly that I strained to hear him over the harp's cascade.

"Cuthbert. Brothers."

"Yes," answered Cuthbert. "We are brothers. We grew together. Learned together. And then we chose our separate paths. I have remained true to mine. So have you. That is why I can do nothing but ensure that you are bound."

If the Piper heard or understood, he gave no sign. He was asleep. He would never know that Cuthbert knelt and kissed him. He would never feel the tear that fell from his brother's eye and glistened on his brow.

50

Alone with Cuthbert

"Your work is complete now, Penelope. The time has come for you to go home."

Cuthbert and I were alone with the sleeping Piper save for the watchful Ulysses, who rested his head on his leg and looked adoringly at his old master. Cuthbert had sent the others outside to wait. Sophy at first had refused to go.

"No, Cuthbert," she said. "I am afraid for Penelope."

"She will be safe. You have my word."

"Come, Sophy," said Alloway, setting down the harp.

"But if you stop playing," she objected, "the Piper will wake and—"

"Sophy," said Cuthbert firmly, "no harm will come to your sister. Penelope has one task still to perform, and there can be no onlookers."

Reluctantly, Sophy took Alloway's arm and led him outside with the others.

"Don't be long, Goose," Scally called.

"You will see her soon, Scallywaggle. And Quentin, please close the door."

Cuthbert and I stood for a moment in silence. There was no sound but the Piper's slow and measured breathing.

"It is a deep sleep," said Cuthbert, finally, "and there is no need to fear his immediate waking."

I watched the Piper's eyes dart beneath their shuttered lids. Already he was dreaming. Already he was traveling.

"Was there no way to save him, Cuthbert?"

"I don't believe that any person can truly save another."

"You saved me."

"You saved yourself, Penelope. And you have found a gift that will sustain you far better than Deep Dreaming, which belongs only to the young. Here you have learned to hear in a way that those who have only their ears will never know. That gift will serve you well as you begin your life as a woman."

There were fragments of mirror scattered all around my feet. I picked up one that was larger than the rest and studied what I could see of my face. Was that a woman? The crazy hair and smudged face? The long scar? I traced it slowly with my finger.

"That scar belongs to Deep Dreaming, Penelope. It won't follow you home."

"But I want to keep it," I said, surprising myself. "As a souvenir. So that I never forget this place and everything that happened here."

"Are you sure?"

"Yes," I answered. And I was.

"You may keep it, then. And now to your final task. You must set the harp you made to playing."

Glass crunched under my sandals as I walked to where the Piper's book lay on the floor. It had fallen open to a page where I read the words, "How to Cause a Conflagration." One glance was all it took for the spell to burn itself into my memory. With this and the spell I had learned in the Piper's fortress, I now owned two incantations. There remained one more for me to speak.

"Show me where, Cuthbert," I said.

He pointed to a page towards the end of the book. I was surprised at how simple the words were. I said them aloud, as Cuthbert told me I must, then listened amazed as the first of my many harps began to play all on its own. The sound was beautiful. Very, very beautiful.

"How long will it play, Cuthbert?"

His smile when he answered was tender and sad. "As long as your heart goes on beating, Penelope, the harp will continue to play."

"You mean that when I—"

He raised his hand to silence me.

"You have many, many years ahead of you. And now your work is complete. The time has come for you to wake."

"But what about Alloway and Sophy? What about the others?"

"They must return the old-fashioned way. On foot."

"How will they know the way?"

"They will manage, I feel sure. They have a long journey ahead of them, but Ulysses will serve as their guide."

The dog whined and looked up at Cuthbert.

"No, Ulysses. Alloway will be your master now. There is nothing for you to do here, and he has need of you."

Ulysses rose slowly. He stretched, as if to bow one last time before the one he loved best. Then he turned tail and went to sit by the door.

"But Cuthbert. What will happen to you?"

"I will have my occupation," he answered, smiling. "I can't think of a better house to haunt than this one. And now, Penelope, truly you must hurry. Farewell. And thank you."

And for the first and only time in my life, I kissed a ghost.

"Farewell, Cuthbert."

I turned my back on the brothers, turned my back on the ringing harp. I opened the door and followed Ulysses into the hall, pulling the door gently closed behind me. Quentin and Scally were waiting.

"Are we done then, Goose?"

"Very nearly."

Ulysses trotted on by and made for the stairs. He was halfway to the front door when he turned and galloped back up the stairs towards us. He stood on his hind legs and licked me from chin to forehead. He bade the same fond adieu to Quentin and to Scally, who was so surprised he didn't have the presence of mind to hiss out his usual objections. Then, with a final wag of his tail, Ulysses was gone.

"My stars and garters," said Scally as he dabbed at the slobber on his whiskers.

"Here," said Quentin, reaching into his pouch and pulling out the neatly folded square that had once been Machalus.

"Dry yourself with this. And you must keep it, Penelope. Something to remind you of me."

I hugged him tight and choked back my tears. Quentin began to sob so loudly that I feared he might wake the Piper.

"Thank you, Quentin, for everything. You have been so brave!"

"I wish we could stay together," he bawled.

"I wish the same. But you belong among dragons, and I belong in Hamelin. We both must go home."

"Do you think we could meet now and then for a skipping contest?" he asked, sniffling.

"I don't think that could be easily arranged," I answered, "though nothing would make me happier. You know how much I love to win a skipping contest."

His tears dried so quickly a hot wind might have blown through the house.

"You won once, true enough. But I've been practicing, and I don't think you'd best me again."

With a sly glance at me, he took his rope and began to jump, right there in the hallway.

Jump! My name is Quentin.
Sugar, pepper, salt.
Here's the skip to take me home:
A triple somersault!

Once, twice, three times he spun around in the air, and then, with a shout of triumph, he vanished.

"Show-off!" I shouted, but he was nowhere near to hear.

"Well," said Scally. "That's that, then."

"I suppose it is."

"Shall we go, Goose?"

"Yes. Are you ready, Scally?"

"Ready."

I took up my skipping rope and sang my rhyme.

Clouds turn into rainstorms, oceans turn to foam,
Count aloud the years since you've been home.
Scissors, rocks and paper, needles, threads and pins
Scallywaggle, Scallywaggle, now come in!

And so it was we came back home. I have lived here ever since.

51

The End

My dear Penelope:

At last I am done. Your harp is ready. I hope you like the case I have made for it. You will never have seen fabric like this before. So strong, so light, so durable. I think you will understand what it is.

"Marry me."

That is what the Shadow has just asked.

"Marry me."

"Shadow. Would that make you happy?"

"Happier than anything in the world."

"And would that keep you quiet?"

"If you married me, you would not mind my talking."

"I am 101 years old, Shadow. Don't you think that is rather old for marrying?"

"It is the perfect age. No one should marry until she knows herself."

"Ah. That is true. Tell me, Shadow. If I were to marry you, could I wear a periwinkle dress?"

"Whatever you would like, Penelope."

"After Penelope and Micah come for their harp, Shadow. I will give you my answer then."

Soon you will come, Penelope. I will give you your harp, and I will give you these words. Perhaps, before you reach the end of them, you will hear the rumor of what has happened, to me, to my house, to all of my harps. People will shake their heads. They will say, "Poor old Harpy. There was no way to save her. It was a terrible fire. The house went up like a tinderbox. All those harps. A lot of kindling. How old was she? A hundred and one if she was a day. What was her name? Why, I can't think. There was some kind of story about her, but I forget what it was. My mother told me part of it when I was a child. Prudence? Persephone? Was her name Persephone? Yes. I think so. Poor old Harpy."

Soon you will come, Penelope, and after you leave the Shadow will return for his answer. I have made up my mind. I know what I will tell him. The fate of Mellon will be my last decision. Should I, or shouldn't I? Perhaps when you hear the news of what has happened to me, you will come to see for yourself. And if you see a great fat rat scuttling among the ash, look at him carefully. You will know who he is.

Good-bye, Penelope. I wish you every good thing. I wish you happiness. I wish you a long, full life. I wish you many dreams. I know you will have them. I knew from the first moment I saw you.

Her name was Penelope. So is mine. Not a day goes by that I don't bless her for the gift of her beloved Alloway. I have cursed her as well, for the harp was not all she bestowed on me. Once she was gone, my own adventures began. At first, I would ask her angry questions. I would speak to her as if she were with me in the room. Sometimes, she would answer. I would hear her clearly, though not with my ears. I would hear her in my heart.

"Why me? Why must I finish what you started, all those years ago?"

"It is not a question of finishing. For some things, there can be no ending."

"What things?"

"Dreaming. Goodness. Evil."

"But how will I know what to do, or where to go? Who will help me?"

"It will be for you as it was for me, Penelope. You will know when you get there. You will find companions along the way. It will be the same for whoever follows after you."

And so it was. And so, I feel sure, it shall be.

Her name was Penelope. She was 101 years old. Now, so am I. I have kept her words to myself for ninety years. It pleased me, somehow, that they belonged to me alone. Ninety years. It is long enough. It is time for me to pass on her story. It will soon be time for me to tell my own.

Whoever reads this, wherever you are, take these words. They are yours. Now you know where the first Penelope went. You know what she did. You know almost everything about her. How she answered the Shadow I think you can guess. And Mellon? I could tell. But of course I won't. Everyone deserves to have at least one secret that outlives her. And that, I believe, is the one she will own forever and ever.